CHASING

A Story of Food, Faith, Fraud and the Pursuit of Longevity

120

Published by Plain Truth Ministries, Pasadena, CA

Unless otherwise indicated, all Scripture passages are from
the Holy Bible, New International Version (NIV) copyright ©1973,
1978, 1984, 2011 by International Bible Society.
Used by permission of Zondervan Publishing House. All
rights reserved.

Library of Congress Cataloging-in-Publication Data

Monte Wolverton. 1948 -
Chasing 120 / Monte Wolverton

p. cm.
Includes biographical references and index.

Cover by iStockphoto/Panagiota Panos and Marv Wegner
ISBN-978-1-889973-15-9

1. Fiction
2. Popular works
3. Christianity—Miscellanea
I. Title

CONTENTS

Prologue:

Your 15-mile drive into the Cascade foothills from downtown Vancouver, Washington has been de-stressing. Office buildings and charming Victorian houses have given way to boxy WW2 era homes and miniature strip malls, which have given way to megastores and suburban developments, which give way to stretches of farmland and forest. You drive up a road which until some years ago had been off limits to the public—a former military training camp. Now, miles into the woods, you find yourself in a quiet, but surprisingly civilized, little valley. You park your car in the expansive, paved lot and look around.

You see dozens of attractive cottages and what appears to be a handsome auditorium. Walkways are filled with busy people and an occasional electric cart. But for some reason your interest is diverted to the fence on the opposite side of the lot, where you spot an unobtrusive rolling gate. Curious, you walk toward it. Although the gate is equipped with a cardkey lock, it has been left ajar. At first you see nothing special on the other side, yet on closer inspection a paved walkway disappears into the bushes and around a large rocky outcrop. You slip through the gate, and after only a few steps you're on a well-maintained trail—wide enough for service vehicles. Still curious, you continue your hike. After a half-mile or so, you are in an increasingly narrow canyon lined with rugged walls of ancient igneous basalt. You encounter another cardkey gate, this one of heavy wrought iron, also left ajar. Security is lax here, you think. Past that, after another quarter mile or so, you arrive in a box canyon, with a waterfall cascading down the far end. Up ahead, you see that the trail ends at the entrance to something like an ancient mine, framed by heavy wooden beams. You

4

approach the entrance, but just inside you encounter a massive camo-green steel door punctuated with large rivets, looking to be of early Cold War vintage. The steel frame sports a cardkey receptacle, obviously a later addition. But again, you don't need to use it, because the door is ajar just enough to get your fingers in. You pull, expecting resistance, but to your surprise the door quietly swings open with hardly any effort, as if its weight has somehow been counterbalanced.

Once inside, you are surprised to find yourself in a clean, brightly lit office environment, at the head of a long central corridor. Men and women in white lab coats cross the corridor on the way from one room to another, sometimes carrying clipboards or laptops, sometimes carrying racks of test tubes or Petri dishes. No one seems to notice you. Is this a dream? Are you invisible? Curious, you walk a little way down the corridor and enter one of the rooms. Two men and a woman, scientists or researchers of some kind, sit at a conference table. At this point you had better be invisible, or security will be on you like bran on whole wheat. Actually, your invisibility probably started back in the parking lot—otherwise security cameras would have tracked you all the way. You sit down in a corner and listen. Then you move in closer because the people are talking barely above a whisper.

"I just don't like it. It's too risky," says the woman.

"I understand your concern," answers the older, gray-haired man, "and believe me I've had the same anxieties over the years. But we've never, ever, had a problem. And if we came close it isn't as though anyone would notice. These are naturally occurring compounds found in a variety of plants sold in supermarkets every day."

"Yes, but not in these concentrations."

"Of course, and that's the question we're trying to answer here."

"Maybe we should hold off, pending more preliminary tests. What I see here is not really definitive," comments the second, younger man, rummaging through a clipboard of papers.

"Well, as always, we would like to see these things to be more definitive, but this is definitive enough, in my judgment. At this point we are talking about subtleties—differences that show up only in test results—five points here or there—at the most, ten or fifteen."

"But still, wouldn't it be better to err on the side of caution?" the woman insists.

"Okay, okay, look," says the older man, leaning back in his chair. "My problem—our problem—is that he wants to test-market this in late fall, and do a roll-out by early spring. That's really pushing our work here. And that's pushing our indoor growing facilities, to say nothing of our farms. That means we need to get our part done by the end of the summer."

"I still don't feel right about it," says the lady, shaking her head and looking down at the table.

"Just remember what we're doing here, Lisa. Think of the big picture. Longevity. We're giving people longer life. And even if we're not quite there yet, we're improving what life they have—or at least helping them believe it's better. I for one feel good about that. And I for one feel it's worth a small risk. And I do mean small."

"So we proceed?" asks the younger man.

"We proceed."

As the meeting breaks up and the researchers—if that's what they are—go their separate ways, you follow the woman down the corridor. She turns into a room with a large glass window in the opposite wall. Through the windows you see long tables holding trays filled with soil and small plants—it looks like they might be some type of fern. Scores of fluorescent UV grow-lights hang from the ceiling. The woman sits down in front of a computer screen.

You wander out of the room and further down the corridor. Another door is open and you hear voices from within. You step inside. While there seems to be plenty of ventilation, the air in this room carries the distinctive odor of rodent urine and wood shavings. Sure enough, the room is lined with cages containing two or three white rats in each—sleeping, eating, and sniffing around. The center of the room holds what appear to be testing devices—a rather large maze, cages with tunnels, doors and switches. Four researchers are gathered around one cage.

"I don't know when this happened," one says. "They seemed fine earlier today. I've checked the records and the dosages were right on the money."

"Maybe this batch was tainted," comments another researcher.

"I'm having that checked, and I've drawn blood on all three. We'll have numbers within the hour."

You draw closer and peek over the researchers' shoulders. In the cage are three white rats—except two appear to be dead—no—they're breathing—perhaps comatose. The third one is waddling frantically around the cage in aimless circles. It's time for you to go. You know these kinds of tests are conducted every day for perhaps hundreds of products that you eat, wear and put on your skin. You know it's necessary and it's better the rats than you, but you just don't like to think about defenseless little creatures suffering so you can use deodorant safely.

So you leave—back up the corridor, out through the heavy steel door, down the trail, through the gates and back to the parking lot. All the time wondering exactly what they were testing on those poor, miserable rats.

CHAPTER ONE

Purveyor

"Five … four … three … two …"

Agrinning face appeared on the screen. It was a lean, mature face with chiseled features, a strong jaw and a luxuriant head of hair, graying around the temples. The face radiated confidence and energy. The grin was insistent, and the steely blue eyes pierced through the camera lens, the image sensor, wires, cable, antennas and out to millions of screens in living rooms across the country.

"And a very good morning to you all!" boomed a rich voice from the grinning mouth, tinged with a gentle Texas twang. "I'm Dr. Tyler Belknap and this is *The 120 Club!*"

Dr. Tyler Belknap's studio operations were impeccable. Morning after morning his staff made sure every detail was in order. All Belknap had to do was show up an hour before the shoot, review his script, briefly meet his guests and, once the cameras were running, let his charm, charisma and grin ooze forth.

The 120 Club was the flagship of Belknap's media efforts. It was really more of an infomercial than a program, as it generated new customers for his Wellness 120 Health Products, new students for his Wellness 120 Institute and new readers for his books. Without

it, sales would lag, and the enthusiasm of his followers would wane. People were not so much buying the
products as they were buying Belknap. He *was* the
brand.

"In a perfect world," began Belknap, "you and I
would enjoy 120 years of happy, abundant, prosperous
life—just as God promised in Genesis 6:3—'And the
Lord said, My spirit shall not always strive with man,
for that he also is flesh: yet his days shall be an hundred and twenty years.' After that, we would all peace-
fully fall asleep and pass into the light. That's what
God wants for every one of us—but we may not be
working with him on this—and that's why you all don't
live 120 years—that's why you are sick—that's why you
are poor—and that's why you suffer."

It wasn't easy to get tickets to be in the studio audience for Belknap's show. Belknap insisted on having
150 people on the other side of the cameras, because
he spoke with more conviction when he had a crowd
in front of him. Applicants had to fill out a form and
attach a recent photograph. The group had to be primarily young, enthusiastic and always fit and attractive—sending the message that his products and practices would make his followers fit and attractive. It was
an unspoken rule that no disabled or unattractive people would be included (unless of course they were featured guests who had been, or needed to be cured of
some problem). People of color were strategically sprin-
kled through the audience to show Belknap's inclusiv-
ity. A few healthy-looking seniors were also important
to show that people were aging well on Belknap products—but certainly no one who looked frail, weak or
even uncomfortable.

It was time for Belknap's sidekick, Sam Patrick, to
prompt him with a question. Sam was a jovial middle-

aged fellow with a fine broadcast voice whose job it was to keep the conversation moving and be a bit of a comic punching bag for his boss. His receding hairline and slightly thicker waistline made Belknap look all the more trim and vital. Yet far from being a lackey, in real life Sam was Chief Financial Officer of Belknap's organization. "Good morning, Dr. Belknap! What a great day to be healthy. And may I say you're looking especially fit today!"

"Good morning, Sam! You're not looking too bad yourself. A little more of my *Weight-Off Elixir* and you'd look even better!"

"Ho ho ho!" guffawed Sam. "You got me there. I just may have a glassful for lunch. That stuff is gooo-ood! And it works! But you know, when you were talking about suffering, I was reminded that so many people believe suffering is just a part of this life. That you have to suffer. That you have to put up with disease, ill health and financial hardship. That you learn through suffering. And that's just soooo wrong, isn't it, Dr. Belknap?"

The technical director switched to a shot of a grinning audience, nodding enthusiastically—then in to a tight shot of Belknap as he spoke.

"That's right, Sam. Look," Belknap leaned into the camera, the grin replaced by an expression of intense sincerity, "you show me someone who's suffering, and I'll show you someone who hasn't kept all of *The Eleven Laws of Wellness*! But what if I could also show you how you could stop suffering and start living a real abundant life? What if I could show you exactly where you could get all the quality food and supplements you need to live longer and happier? What if I could show you a network of friends all across the country who will gladly come up alongside you to help you as you discover genuine wellness?"

The camera pulled back from the tight shot of Belknap to reveal a mature man sitting across the table from him, beside Sam. His hair was appliance white and his face revealed the character of advanced age, while seeming to radiate health and energy.

"I'd like you all to meet a dear friend of mine," beamed Belknap. "Believe it or not, Harry Summers is 102 years old. Imagine that! How have you kept so fit and vibrant, Harry?"

"Well, Dr. Belknap, I actually owe it all to you." Harry's voice was not the shaky, hoarse intonation you would expect from someone of that age, but a rich, clear baritone—Belknap's grin turned sheepish and he patted Harry's mottled but strong hand. "I appreciate that Harry, but I have to give credit to God for the secrets that he has revealed to me. Harry, why don't you tell us your story?"

Harry did. Like thousands of others, he had heard Dr. Belknap on TV years before. In his 70s, he had begun to have a few health problems, which gradually worsened over the years—diabetes, gout, gallstones—even a couple of bouts with cancer. On top of all that, his memory was failing. He was discouraged—as he felt the end of his life was near. Then in his early 80s he had started using Dr. Belknap's products, and his health improved—a little at first, then dramatically. His memory and mental sharpness came back with a vengeance. Since that time he had been active, golfing and jogging daily, and, having outlived his first two wives, was dating a spunky 72-year-old.

"Belknap grinned, chuckled and patted Harry's hand again. "Ho ho ho ho ho," boomed Sam. The director cut to the studio audience, who were laughing, smiling and gaping in awe at the incredibly healthy centenarian.

"Isn't that just a wonderful story?" enthused Belknap. "Let's give Mr. Summers a hand." The audience joined Belknap in energetic applause.

"You know, friends, Mr. Summers here is easily headed toward 120. Easily. If you want to be like him—if you want to see your great, great grandkids—if you want to grow old without all the problems that we have been told have to come with age—I invite you to drop in to any of our Wellness 120 stores—or visit any branch of our Wellness 120 Institute in a city near you—or call the toll-free number on your screen right now."

The director cut to a panning overhead shot of a cheering audience with Belknap, Summers and Sam still on the set, then cut back to the grinning Belknap, who turned to his sidekick.

"You know, Sam, the laws of wellness aren't just for older people. They start applying to you from the very time you are conceived."

"No question about that, Dr. Belknap. In fact, here at the Wellness 120 Institute we have great programs for young people. And today we just happen to have with us three outstanding kids, randomly selected from the big group at our Wellness 120 Institute in Cincinnati."

Two boys and a girl, all well scrubbed, wholesome and 15 years old, stepped confidently onto the stage. Belknap motioned for them to sit on a couch. The audience thundered and cheered. Belknap invited them to introduce themselves and give brief bios.

"Three years ago when I was in middle school," offered Meghan, "I felt like I was on a roller coaster all the time. I drank pop all day and maybe an energy drink. I would be wired for a while and then totally crash. I was feeling sick a lot. I had, like, complexion problems and I was depressed. I screamed at my parents sometimes, and I was getting into fights at school. I just wasn't happy."

"And then what happened?" Belknap prompted.

"Okay, one day my mom started watching you on TV and she started changing the stuff we ate. At first I didn't like it, but then I started feeling a little better. Pretty soon I started feeling good. She took me down to the Wellness 120 Institute and there were a bunch of other kids there in these classes where we learned how to cook healthy food and take supplements and stuff. And now I feel great all the time."

"And where do you think all that stuff came from?" prompted Belknap, again.

"I dunno—from you?"

Lots of laughter from the audience. "Ho ho ho ho ho ho ho," intoned Sam.

"Well—heh heh," grinned Belknap, "actually, I was merely led to discover things that others had not seen before."

More applause and cheering from the audience.

"Sam, aren't these young people wonderful? You know," Belknap continued, "frankly, the trouble with young people we've had in this country since the 1960s can be laid at the door of poor nutrition—kids and their parents just not following *The Eleven Laws of Wellness*. And here, right before your eyes, is an example of what a big difference those principles can make.

"My friends, these young folks right here are literally the future of our country. Today, if you go to the fast food outlets and supermarkets to feed your family, you will get food filled with toxic chemicals, preservatives, pesticides and growth hormones. You will get unclean meat that God never intended for us to consume. You will get horrible *genetically modified foods* that God never intended humankind to eat. You and billions of other unsuspecting people will have no resistance against the terrifying mutant disease epidemics that are coming.

"And make no mistake about it—refined and genetically modified food will cause your spirit to become *perverse.* It's why so many people today are afflicted with and possessed by perversity of spirit! If you don't believe me, just look at the world around you! Most of the world's medical professionals, psychologists, politicians, scientists and even preachers and theologians don't understand these principles!

"But here you see the results of Wellness 120 products—people of advanced age enjoying robust, abundant living and sharp, clear minds—young people whose bodies and minds are unpolluted by toxic chemicals and wrong-headed foods—people who are safe from the coming catastrophe because they have stocked up on our wonderful freeze-dried *Wellness 120 Survival Packages*—which can keep you and your family healthy during the perilous end times while everyone else around you is dying from the horrible pandemics that are just around the corner!

"And may I remind you that every last one of my Wellness 120 foods, products and supplements are one hundred percent organic, *one hundred percent sustainable and one hundred percent GMO free! As God intended from the beginning!*

"Do the people on this stage look like they have a spirit of perversity? I should say not! Good food has made them healthy, righteous and godly! And I guarantee you that some day young men and women just like these will be the ones to clean it all up and bring about a sparkling new world—mark my words!"

———⟫●⟪———

Another huge media campaign was coming down

the pike. Dave Whitman could feel it. As Creative Director at Wellness 120, he had worked his way through scores of them over the years. Again and again, Whitman had seen Belknap get a bee in his bonnet—a Big Idea that would grab the public interest, increase sales at retail outlets, galvanize his followers and sell more of his books. And nine times out of ten, Belknap was right on target.

As usual, this one was consistent with Belknap's style, forged during his years as marketing director for a powerful Los Angeles media company. *Where did your health go? What happened to all the energy and good looks you had in high school? Did you know there's no reason why you can't stay fit, healthy and energetic until you're 120 years old? You can—if you know the ancient health secrets revealed in my book! You won't find them anywhere else!*

Belknap would expect visual concepts within a week along with copy for print, Internet, radio and direct mail—as well as storyboards for TV ads. Whitman asked his assistant Velma to set up a time for an initial brainstorming meeting with his art directors and copywriters.

And then there was Clifford Bartlett. Whitman always liked to have Bartlett along for the ride, because he always brought a new perspective to the table. An African American, Bartlett was probably the best scholar in Belknap's organization—an advisor and resource for several departments, Academic Dean of the Wellness 120 Institute and member of the Board of Directors. Since hiring on to Belknap's group some 15 years ago, he had earned two PhDs from Columbia University. Belknap's credibility was bolstered when his staff had that kind of credentials. Bartlett seemed dedicated, although he certainly didn't fit the mold of the organization man. To Whitman's way of thinking, Bartlett was a genuine Christian.

But sometimes Bartlett was hard to read. Occasionally, and privately, he had been known to express doubt about some of Belknap's ideas. Yet he always took his well-aimed shots in an enigmatically non-threatening way. A cleverly designed ambiguity often makes the best duck-blind.

———⟫●⟪———

In 1991, Marcia Whitman was dead tired all the time. Some days she could barely get out of bed. She had used up all the available sick leave at the mortgage company where she was beginning a promising career as an underwriter. She hadn't been to work in two weeks. Had she been three or four decades older, maybe she would have chalked it up to aging—but she was only 22. She and Dave, a young and ambitious graphic designer, had been married only a year. She wasn't pregnant. So far, her doctor hadn't been able to identify any reason for her debilitating lack of energy. In the early '90s a few enlightened physicians understood this to be chronic fatigue syndrome, but the causes were not clear and the disease was only beginning to be accepted by the mainstream medical profession. Marcia had begun looking to alternative healing sources for answers.

Not that her husband wasn't concerned about her—he was. But he was also immersed in his work—and Marcia tended to be more proactive about health matters. One of the Portland, Oregon UHF TV stations was big on health infomercials and programs. For a week or two, Marcia had dragged herself to the living room at 8 am to glean what she could from these sometimes-bizarre teachers. Then one day a new infomercial was added to the mix—*The 120 Club* with some guy named Tyler Belknap. At first Marcia distrusted him. He looked a little too robust. Worse yet—he seemed to have a strong Bible-based component to his ideas. Marcia, like her husband, was a nominal Christian but she didn't want to get involved with any kind of oddball group. Still, she tuned in day after day to see what Belknap had to say.

Health, he said, was a matter of obedience to a set of laws he had discovered in the Bible. Once you understood and obeyed those laws, you could claim the promise found in Genesis 6:3 and live a vigorous, robust life until the age of 120. Because humanity as a whole had not lived in obedience to these laws, explained Belknap, everyone was sick—and big trouble was coming soon. Toxic chemicals, preservatives, pesticides and processed foods along with new and frightening mutant diseases would combine to bring catastrophic epidemics. Those who survived would be those who had lived in accord with the Bible's wellness laws. They would be on the ground floor of a healthy new world— a world of vibrant men, women and children living life to the full.

Dr. Belknap, a mere 61 years old, had accumulated a small group of remarkably well-preserved seniors—living testimonials for his products and teachings—the "Methuselah League." These loyal men and women, all approaching or over the age of 90, happily endorsed everything Belknap said or did. He trotted them out as often as he could on his show and infomercials.

Marcia wasn't sure about the new world thing, but Belknap's ideas about health seemed sound. And she had nothing to lose by trying a few of his products. His *Methuselah Tea* seemed interesting, as well as his *120 Blood Cleanser*. She would give it a month. If nothing happened, she would resume her search elsewhere.

In the next month, Marcia gave it the best she could. Dave was busy with several projects, so he didn't have time to participate. But if it made Marcia feel better, he was okay with it. She avoided white flour, sugar, coffee, chocolate, pork and shellfish. She ate raw kale, and snacked on whole organic barley. She walked five miles a day. She read as many of Tyler Belknap's books as she could get her hands on—including *Five Things God Really Hates About You and How You Can Fix Them, Deadly Pandemics Are Coming—How You Can Escape, Make God Happy by Obeying His Health Laws, How GMOs and White Sugar Will Pervert Your Spirit* and *You Can Live to Be 120!* She consumed his products and supplements.

And then an incredible thing happened. She felt better. Not just better but really, really better. Her energy returned. Her mental acuity was better than it had been in months. She believed she had been healed because of Tyler Belknap.

Dave couldn't help but notice the change in his wife, but he tended to be more skeptical about alternative medicine, herbal remedies, faith healers and the like.

"Aren't you being a little hasty?" queried Dave. "There are half a dozen other variables that could have contributed to your feeling better."

"Dave—I know my own body—and I just have a strong feeling that these remedies somehow made a difference, and that Dr. Belknap knows what he's talking about. And you know that problem you've been having with allergies? Why don't you try Belknap's *Anti Allergy Answer* for just two weeks and see if that helps."

"Marcia, I don't think..."

"Dave..."

Whitman could never pass up a challenge—especially from his wife. "Okay. You're on."

He ordered a bottle of the little green capsules—and diligently popped them for two weeks. To his surprise, the sneezing and watery eyes that had bothered him were gone.

Marcia and Dave devoured Belknap's books as well as his supplements. They began attending classes at Belknap's Wellness 120 Institute—classes about biblical calisthenics, godly food preparation, yucca fasting and a timetable for the coming apocalypse. The people seemed helpful, supportive and down-to-earth.

One day an instructor called Dave aside. "You know—there's an opening for an art director at Dr. Belknap's headquarters. You should apply. It's right here in the Portland area so you won't need to relocate. And I know you'll feel like you're part of something much bigger than yourself."

Whitman frowned. His ad agency job was going really well. He was proud of his work—had even won a couple of industry awards. But maybe it was time to get into something more meaningful—something that would really make a difference.

The next week he got an appointment and showed up, portfolio and resumé in hand, at Belknap's impressive headquarters overlooking the Columbia River east of Vancouver, Washington. After a brief meeting in HR, he was ushered into the office of the VP of Operations, Carlton Vance. Whitman had been in ad agencies and other companies many times larger than Belknap's—but he had never, anywhere, seen a desk the size of Vance's. With the addition of a couple of Pratt and Whitney jet engines, the desk looked like it might be airworthy. And the man behind it had the crisp demeanor of an experienced Dreamliner pilot. Vance leaned across the polished teak expanse to shake Whitman's hand.

"I understand you're quite the up-and-coming designer. I see some big clients on your resumé."

"Yes, thank you sir. I've had some excellent opportunities and some good teachers," answered Whitman, with efface.

"I'm glad to hear you say that, Dave, because if we make an offer and you accept, you have to realize that we have our own culture and style here. You may have to unlearn a few habits you formed out there in the world's advertising business."

"Um—the world?—well, I guess I sort of assumed you would be making your decision based on my experience and qualifications, which as you can see are…"

"I'll be frank with you Dave. When we hire 'professionals,' we aren't much interested in their creative opinions and ideas about what our promotions should look like. Dr. Belknap has plenty of experience in that regard. He knows exactly what he wants. What we want is your nuts-and-bolts abilities to produce clean, attractive pages that let the Belknap style shine through. You need to understand that right up front."

"Certainly, and I…"

"We'll pay you a salary that is consistent with what you made on the outside—maybe even a little more. We value loyalty. And we value flexibility."

Whitman had expected more of an examination and discussion of his portfolio. But it was clear that this was a different kind of company. It sounded like they wanted him to shut up and work—for a higher salary than he was making at the agency. He didn't quite understand how a relatively new organization like Belknap's could afford to pay better than what he was making at the agency, and for that matter he couldn't understand why they were spending so darn much on office appointments and desks. But they must be doing something right. What was the worst thing that could happen? His portfolio might suffer a bit—but if it got too weird, and if it became evident that he was not developing as a professional designer, he could always quit and jump back into the ad business.

Whitman accepted the offer. That had been twenty years ago. Whitman, and later his staff, had taken the "Belknap style," and morphed it into a sophisticated, clever and trendy media presence envied by the best advertising professionals. When they all moved into the new office building, Carlton Vance had gained an even more impressive office. And Dave Whitman, as Creative Director, was sitting in his own posh office behind that huge flying desk.

CHAPTER TWO

Quandary

Sometimes Whitman wondered about Belknap. Belknap wasn't "churchy," and that was just fine for Whitman, who had never identified in the least with popular Evangelical culture. All the bizarre language, whiny self-absorption, sanctimonious hand gestures and outlandish emotionalism (not to mention the outright denial of science) left him cold. Why would God—the most intelligent being in the universe—be pleased with any of that? That's why, in spite of his initial skepticism about Belknap, Whitman had eventually come to appreciate the culture of the organization. Belknap used some religious language—enough to engage the nominally Christian market. But for the most part, he came across as matter-of-fact and to the point. He was more of a salesman than a preacher. Whitman certainly had no problem with that approach. But there were other things about Belknap and the organization that secretly nagged at him.

People living to be 120 years old? Did Whitman actually believe this stuff? Well—maybe he did at one time. Did he actually know of anyone who had lasted for 120 years? No, but, as Belknap had explained many times, that's because nobody really had kept all the health laws perfectly except maybe the patriarchs of the Bible and other holy men of old—and that's why they lived so long. Jesus also kept the health laws perfectly. He was crucified in his 30s—but his body was so full of energy that he was able to resurrect himself, Belknap explained. Yes, it took a lot of work, yet if you made the effort, God *had* to reward you, because he had promised to in Genesis, or so Belknap taught.

What about the people who seemed to keep all the laws and died in an accident—or got cancer—or died of a heart attack? Well, maybe those folks had some secret sins—like midnight munchies when they scarfed down cookies and ice cream. Or maybe earlier in their lives they had messed up their health so much that keeping the laws of wellness couldn't save them.

In any case, years ago, Dave and Marcia had grown out of their true-believer, check-your-brains-at-the-door phase. They weren't exactly disloyal. They were just realists. The Whitmans believed they had a balanced perspective on Belknap. They understood that Belknap was human and some of his ideas were a bit off the wall, and that he had kind of a cult following, but they also thought the organization was doing good work—keeping people healthy. What could be wrong with that?

After all, if you took a survey of people who followed (or worked for) charismatic teachers, you would probably come up with a bell-shaped curve. On the one extreme you would likely find people who worship the leader and believe he or she can do no wrong. On the other extreme you would find skeptics. In the center you might find people like the Whitmans. And now even they were sliding toward the skeptical end of the curve.

Another of the Whitmans' concerns was that Belknap seemed to have set Jesus on a back burner. Belknap talked about Jesus, to be sure, but he had redesigned his Jesus to suit himself. Belknap portrayed Jesus as a pragmatic, no-nonsense, businesslike CEO—a perfectly fit, ruggedly athletic, hyperactive Jesus-on-the-go.

Ironically, given the popular alternatives (the saccharine mainstream Protestant Jesus, the nutty charismatic Jesus, and the dour Catholic Jesus) the Whitmans found Belknap's idea of a businesslike Jesus attractive, for the most part.

But wasn't Jesus supposed to be much more than that—wasn't Jesus the Way, the Truth and the Life? Sometimes it seemed to Dave and Marcia that Belknap was selling his *own* way, truth and life—which was nothing more than a collection of routines, rules and regulations that needed to be followed.

Dave's other main target of increasing skepticism was Belknap's "end times" narrative. His ideas about people taking over the world as a reward for eating right and adhering to *The Eleven Principles of Wellness* seemed to make little sense, in light of what Whitman knew about the Bible. And Belknap's thing about "perversity of the spirit"—evil spirits influencing you just because you ate a candy bar—that was just bizarre. And what kind of Christian would sit idly by, munching on his secret cache of freeze-dried whole-grain snacks, while his neighbors were dying of hunger and end-time disease epidemics?

So far, Dave and Marcia hadn't discussed these concerns with anyone else. Belknap didn't put up with dissent in his organization, and Dave didn't want to put his job in jeopardy. So they continued to watch—and think. In spite of the cynicism that had crept into Dave and Marcia's thinking in the last five years (along with the ability to keep it discreetly hidden), Dave just kept on doing his job and Marcia kept on homemaking. Things had turned out well for them, and regardless of the problems, they still fundamentally believed that it was all because Marcia had bought into Tyler Belknap's teaching. Their social network was mostly centered on friends and co-workers at Wellness 120. They were both in good shape physically. They had two smart, healthy kids. They lived in a large, two-story tract home on a quiet cul-de-sac in the upper-middle-class eastern reaches of Vancouver, Washington. They really had little reason to change or to upset any apple carts.

They would find motivation to critically examine their lives in the coming weeks.

Dave and Marcia's son, Jason, announced his arrival with a house-shaking slam of the front door and a rustling thud of his book-laden backpack on the floor. At seventeen, Jason was lanky and athletic—an all-around jock who played center on his basketball team at Union High School—as well as a straight-A student.

A large, thick envelope was laying on the dining room table—addressed to him. Jason picked it up and stared at the return address: "Wellness 120 Institute." A smile spread across his face. He was pretty sure he knew what it was. This would be a great way to spend what might be his last full summer before going off to college next year. He hoped his grades would get him into Stanford University. He was interested in medical research—and intensely interested in an athletic scholarship. In any case, next summer would be frantic and this summer would be his last chance to enjoy the forests of the Pacific Northwest.

Jason tore off the end of the envelope, yanking out the stack of papers inside.

Congratulations! You have been selected to participate in the annual Wellness 120 Institute Summer Pro-

gram at our beautiful Retreat Center, located in the foothills of the Cascade Mountains east of Vancouver, Washington.

"Epic!" Jason shouted to whoever was in the house. "I'm in!"

"In what!" called Marcia from the kitchen.

"The summer program at the Institute!"

"Whoa!" came a girl's voice from upstairs. It was Jason's 11-year-old sister Brandi. "I wish I was going! Cari's sister went last year and she hasn't stopped talking about it. It was so cool. They sent them out in the woods with just a pocketknife, a compass, a roll of string and some energy bars and they had to stay there for like four days. They had to build their own shelters and find their own food and everything."

"That doesn't sound like much fun to me," said Marcia. "Maybe it would have about twenty years ago—before I had you two."

For the past decade the Wellness 120 Institute had put on a three-week summer program for high-school age teens. Hundreds applied—only a hundred were selected. It was different than the local Institute courses. Tuition and expenses were free—covered by the Institute. If this seemed overly generous, it was calculated to appear that way. Among other things, it was a program carefully designed to generate customer loyalty. The limit of one-hundred was based on Defense Department studies on optimal sizes for group bonding, loyalty and combat effectiveness in soldiers. If students at the summer program had a positive experience, built solid friendships and stayed in touch with each other, they would talk it up with their friends and families. You couldn't buy that kind of goodwill. Well, actually Belknap *was* buying it.

Activities included all kinds of sports, hiking, fishing, mountain biking, swimming, archery, marksmanship—and a substantial emphasis on wilderness survival. A wide variety of wholesome foods were provided—along with liberal doses of Belknap's supplements and energy snacks. There were a few classes—but most of the time was spent outside. At the end of the session, students usually went home feeling energized and healthier than ever—indoctrinated and sold on the Wellness 120 brand.

Jason was flipping through the stack of instructions and other papers from the envelope. "Looks like there's some forms and a bunch of legal stuff you need to sign and get back to them by next week."

Marcia picked up the forms and started skimming through them. A letter to parents or guardians assured them that, although the agreement was filled with frightening legalese, it was merely a formality required by the organization's liability insurance underwriters. *Rest assured, your child will have the time of his or her life.* Finally, Marcia scanned the agreement itself, which asked parents for permission to give their child medical treatment in the event such treatment was needed *…parent or guardian agrees to hold the Organization harmless for damages or injuries incurred by the attendee in the duration of this program.*

What does that mean? thought Marcia. *They say they will cover medical treatment but then they say the family is responsible for any injuries. That doesn't make sense.*

There was also a strange little phrase that could easily have been glossed over: *Parent or guardian authorizes the Organization to provide, at its sole discretion, dietary supplements and foods for attendee. Secondary effects may vary.*

Marcia was put off by the defensive and obfuscating tone of the document, but she didn't say anything to Jason. He was still on a high—and frantically texting his friends to see if anyone else he knew had been accepted.

Dave arrived home about 5:30 and Jason let him know the news the minute he got in the door. "That's great, son! You're gonna love it. Plus, you get a certificate, don't you? Which will be another impressive thing to put on your Stanford application."

After dinner Marcia showed Dave the legal documents. "Hmm," pondered Dave. "Yeah, it does sound kind of defensive. But on the other hand, I've worked with the guys in legal for two decades and I'm sure they're just doing what they have to do to cover their buttocks."

"What's up with this thing about supplements and foods? Doesn't that bother you a little?" asked Marcia.

"Maybe. But isn't that just saying that they're going to feed Jason a lot of good stuff and that some foods might disagree with him? I dunno. Why do they even have that in there? Maybe some kids got the runs last year and their parents got upset."

Dave thought for a while. "Look. They've got one staff member for every four students. With all that supervision, how could anything really go wrong? The worst that can happen to Jason is that he sprains an ankle or something—and it says here that any medical care will be provided by the Institute."

"Yes, it says that," Marcia pointed to the next line, "but then right afterward it says we're ultimately responsible—we agree to 'hold the Organization harmless.' I mean, should we even sign this? I really want Jason to go, but…"

"Okay. Okay. I'll admit it sounds defensive and it doesn't make sense. Why don't I do this—why don't I

just ask the legal guys about it in the morning? I'm
sure they'll be able to clarify everything."

⸺➤◆◄⸺

The more he thought about it, the more the word-
ing of the agreement nagged at Whitman. Already he was
doubting things about the organization. He certainly
wanted to believe everything was on the up-and-up, and
that he could trust the company for which he had worked
for 20 years to take care of his son for a few weeks. It was
an over-reaction on his part, he kept telling himself.
The guys in Legal would tell him not to worry. Of course
they would. What else would they tell him? "Sure Dave,
there are, in fact, some serious risks at the Summer Institute. You don't know anything about these risks, but we
were hoping you wouldn't read this too closely so we
could push some of the responsibility for them back to
you." No—his friends in Legal would not say that. They
would tell him, "It's all good! Don't worry about a
thing!" So, thought Dave, there was really no point in
asking his friends in Legal about this at all, was there?

But for the life of him, he couldn't imagine how the
Summer Institute could be a problem. Jason wanted to
go—to keep him from going was out of the question.

At the same time, Dave resolved to do something
he had wanted to do for a long time—find out more
about Belknap's early years.

Enterprise

Everyone who worked at Wellness 120, along with millions of Wellness 120 followers, knew the Belknap story, because Belknap had included it in his first book *The Eleven Laws of Wellness*. The official story went something like this:

John Tyler Belknap was born in 1953 in the east Texas city of Tyler. His parents decided to dub him with the city's namesake, John Tyler—tenth President of the United States. Tyler Belknap, as he preferred to be called, grew up in the small town of Mineola (about 25 miles north of the city of Tyler) for his first 12 years—long enough to permanently instill in him a friendly Texas twang. In 1965 his father took a job in the growing aerospace industry in Southern California. After high school, Tyler quickly earned his PhD and went to work for a big media conglomerate in L.A. For nearly a decade Belknap distinguished himself as a marketing genius.

He earned an impressive salary, lived in Bel Air and drove a Porsche 928 S4. He sent his young kids to the best private schools. He took his family on vacations to Thailand and Monte Carlo.

Then in late 1987 the stock market suffered a downturn and recession followed. The company Belknap worked for was hit hard. In the course of a corporate shakeup the following year, Belknap lost his job. No one was hiring. He found himself deep in debt—he could no longer afford his home, car and lavish lifestyle. He declared bankruptcy. With his family, he endured a period of horrible aimlessness and depression. On top of that, both he and his wife found themselves in failing health. The stress of the situation was taking its toll on them.

Finally, with no pride left, Belknap went hat-in-hand to his brother-in-law Harold, who was at least making ends meet with his family farm in Brush Prairie, Washington, just northeast of Vancouver and north of Portland, Oregon. Belknap asked Harold if he could live on a small corner of his land. Belknap said he would come up with a used trailer somewhere, and find money somehow to dig a well, install a septic tank and eventually bring in electricity. In return for the rent of the land for his trailer to sit on, Belknap would help his brother-in-law run the farm. Maybe the labor and menial chores would give him the focus he needed to sort his life out. And the public schools in that area weren't half bad.

Desperate for hope and encouragement, Belknap turned to the Bible. In the course of his reading, he became enraptured by Genesis 6:3, which seemed to him to guarantee that humans could live as long as 120 years. For six solid months he scoured the Bible for more clues and secrets. He and his wife began practicing the principles he found. Their health improved. Their energy and mental acuity returned. According to Belknap, it was nothing short of a miracle effected by God in return for obedience to biblical health laws.

The result of all this would be Belknap's seminal work, *The Eleven Laws of Wellness*, published in 1990. Using a few of his old marketing connections, he pitched one of the nation's top publishers. The book wasted no time making it to *New York Times* best-seller list, not just because many people would like to live to 120—but also because Belknap knew how to write dramatically, and because he took charge of the book's promotion.

The rest of the story had been made public in scores of newspaper and magazine articles about Belknap and Wellness 120.With revenues and publicity from his book, Belknap opened a small health-food store in Vancouver. In a warehouse behind the store he began manufacturing his own line of supplements. He pitched them to natural food stores in Portland and Seattle. He bought time on local UHF and cable TV channels, promoting his book and supplements on the air. He bought print ads in national publications. He started taking orders on the phone and by mail. He quickly outgrew his warehouse and bought a larger plant. He opened two retail stores in Portland—one on the east side and the other in affluent Lake Oswego. To ensure quality ingredients, he started his own farming operation in eastern Oregon, near Ontario. He offered daily health classes in his stores. In a matter of months there were more students than the stores could accommodate, so he leased separate office space and dubbed it the Wellness 120 Institute.

It was a story of growth that any businessperson would envy—or kill for. And the growth had continued steadily into the 2000s, even surviving the Great Recession with nothing more than a bump. Beyond the success of his company, Belknap had become something of a celebrity. Early on, he had invested a lot of time shaking hands and networking at local chambers of commerce and other business groups. He had people who did that for him now on the local level. Long ago he had attracted the attention of national media—

and was regularly a guest on talk shows. Belknap had become America's number one longevity guru. He made regular trips to Washington DC—developing friendships with several powerful figures in Congress. He was called to testify in congressional hearings on the quality of food in America.

Now, Belknap was headquartered in an impressive office building overlooking the city of Portland and the Columbia River in well-to-do east Vancouver, Washington. He boasted three large plants producing supplements, food items and other health-related products. There was a Wellness 120 retail franchise in nearly every major city in the U.S. and Canada—and some products were available in supermarkets.

And then there was the magnificent Wellness 120 Conference center tucked away in a corner of the old Camp Bonneville in the Cascade foothills. Camp Bonneville had been established in 1909 as a drill field and rifle range for the U.S. Army, stationed some 15 miles west at the Vancouver Barracks. It was used as a training camp for various branches of the military over the years. In 1995, the nearly 4,000-acre camp was closed and acquired by Clark County for use as a park—but not until the Army agreed to pay for cleaning up eight decades of unexploded munitions of all types (except, perhaps, nuclear), and the removal of any other toxic substances contaminating soil and groundwater. That process had taken decades. With the help of his political connections, Belknap acquired a remote portion of the camp—an idyllic little vale nestled among the forested hills west of Larch Mountain.

Belknap and his staff had transformed his acquisition from rugged wilderness into the Wellness 120 Retreat Center—a sort of utopian resort. In the center of the campus sat the handsome Conference Hall designed to hold 800 people, with a kitchen and dining facility connected by breezeways. Bronze sculptures of Old Testament figures dotted the grounds. They weren't the classical robed saints of old biblical paintings—but fit, muscular men and women in dynamic poses looking more like comic book superheroes—illustrating Belknap's biblical vision of wellness. A natural stream stocked with rainbow trout cut through the campus, winding through several ponds, rapids and waterfalls. A helipad lay in a clearing a few hundred yards away. Paved lanes connected the various buildings and electric golf carts whizzed back and forth. Scores of little white cottages poked out of the surrounding forest like the fingertips of colossal giants buried deep within the earth. To the south of the main campus, two large concrete and glass structures jutted out of a forested hill—an administration building and Belknap's retreat residence. A nine-hole golf course stretched off to the west.

The facility hosted multiple functions: Creative retreats for headquarters staff, training sessions for managers, entertainment of new suppliers, distributors and retailers—and of course, schmoozing of political figures by Belknap and his inner circle.

Image was supremely important to Belknap. With the exception of executives and board members with their *de rigueur* suits or jackets (skirts for women), every one of Belknap's employees sported a uniform of some kind, depending on their function and status. Belknap had decided early-on that a certain regimentation was a good idea—it graphically reinforced the concept that Belknap's employees were part of an elite corps—a "chosen" people. The organization's image was further polished and maintained by information officer Dawson Criswell, who crafted press releases daily about new products and new initiatives. If any unpleasantness leaked out, Criswell was a master at spinning it back into the most positive context.

Twenty-three branches of the Wellness 120 Institute dotted North America. Trained instructors taught classes in every aspect of wellness—nutrition, exercise, cooking and physiology—always with Belknap's metaphysical and spiritual spin. There were classes for every age group—or just support groups if customers were so inclined. The net result was loyal buyers who came back again and again. Everyone seemed to agree that from appearances Belknap and his organization were living some kind of charmed life.

But Belknap's teaching was quite another matter. It wasn't so much that anyone had a problem with living a healthy lifestyle, eating more greens, fruits and vegetables, taking a few supplements and getting some exercise. It was all the other baggage. Over the years a few reputable Bible scholars and theologians had offered their opinions. Their consensus was that Belknap's scriptural stylings were laughable at best and destructive at worst.

Likewise, qualified nutritionists and faculty at medical schools were certainly aware of Belknap, but chuckled at some of his pseudo-scientific ideas about nutrition and human physiology. Additionally, the Centers for Disease Control and other experts in the field of epidemiology didn't appreciate Belknap's alarmist ideas about pandemics destroying civilization as we know it.

Belknap's teaching boiled down to five simple concepts:

• Human beings are intended to live to 120 years—or even beyond—if they simply follow the right health principles, i.e. *Belknap's* principles.

• The key to mental, emotional and spiritual clarity is nutrition. The reason so many people are confused, unhappy and spiritually bankrupt is that they don't eat right. Every disease—every mental, emotional and spiritual problem known to man is a result of poor nutrition and failure to abide by *The Eleven Laws of Wellness.*

• Refined and genetically modified foods cause what Belknap called "perversity of the spirit." By this, he meant that demonic spiritual forces were roaming the universe. Poor nutrition opened humans up to these forces. Demons especially love greasy fast food, biblically "unclean" meats such as pork and shellfish, refined white sugar and strong coffee.

• By contrast, healthful eating and regular exercise tunes your mind and spirit. Whole, unrefined foods make one more righteous and godly. Demonic spirits detest organic food and fresh fruits and vegetables. "Eat right and put the devil to flight," was one of Belknap's favorite aphorisms.

• Disease epidemics are on the way. Billions would die, but Belknap offered a way of escape. Those who follow right nutritional practices would survive and help usher in a sparkling, prosperous new world.

Anyone would agree that these ideas were unorthodox—maybe even a bit loony. But in the vast scheme of things—with so many other hucksters out there propagating far more bizarre ideas, the fact that Belknap had a few weird notions, of and by itself, was not that newsworthy. Belknap realized the power of unique, even bizarre, selling propositions. Without his biblical 120 years and his pandemic threats, he would be just another organic pill pusher. And if you repeat any idea often enough, people will believe it.

Any quirkiness was more than offset by the financial success of the enterprise, the carefully cultivated air of legitimacy and charitable involvement. Belknap made sure he was in front of the cameras for local and national disaster relief and charities. His PR and marketing people cranked out a continuous stream of image ads designed to put Belknap and his organization in a warm, glowing light.

To date, Dave Whitman had not spent a lot of time looking into the accuracy of Belknap's personal narrative. But he imagined that as each year passed, the story would be increasingly difficult to verify. The two people who had worked most closely with him in Los Angeles were now his CFO, Sam Patrick, and his VP of Operations, Carlton Vance. Belknap had offered them jobs within a year of opening his first store. Of course, publicly, they had only good things to say about Belknap.

Some 15 years ago Belknap's brother-in-law Harold had passed away and bequeathed his acreage to Belknap, who now used it as pasture for his dairy cattle. Belknap's wife, Lois, never one to talk with the media, had succumbed to undisclosed health challenges 12 years ago. While Belknap had claimed in his first book that Lois had improved, these improvements had turned out to be only temporary. Belknap often commented that she would still be thriving today had he discovered his regimen only a few years earlier.

Organizational scuttlebutt had it that Belknap's son was an investment consultant living in the Cayman Islands. His daughter, with a PhD in Entomology, was living in Panama, studying moths indigenous to the jungles of that country. Neither of them granted interviews about their father, and their father never spoke about them publicly.

Dave and Marcia had scoured the Internet for articles that would give them a clue about Belknap's life in Southern California during the 80s. There were a few.

In rare interviews, men and women who interacted with him then remembered him to be thoroughly professional—an ambitious, driven young man. But the closer people had been to Belknap in those years, the less it seemed they were inclined to talk about him now.

One element that particularly tantalized the Whitmans was the pains Belknap took to guard the formulas for his products. Over the years Dave had learned from various coworkers how Wellness 120 production processes were compartmentalized in the same way the federal government had compartmentalized the development of the atomic bomb. Ingredients for any given product were pre-mixed by different teams at different sites, so that the final team didn't know what was in the finished item. Carlton Vance kept the only hard-copy list of product ingredients in a safe in his office—backed up by encrypted digital files stored at locations known only to Vance, Patrick and Belknap.

The Whitmans couldn't help but wonder—did Belknap really believe and practice what he preached? From all appearances, Belknap seemed to be a disciplined man. He jogged four miles daily—rain, shine or snow. He avoided white sugar and ate meat only sparingly, and then only organic and free range—and nothing prohibited by the dietary regulations found in Leviticus 11. He ate mostly fruits, vegetables and whole grains—all of them organic and non-GMO. He drank a glass of red wine every day from his own organic vineyards. He drank only one cup of coffee a day—always organic. He took a daily regimen of supplements. As much as possible, he used foods and products prepared and sold in his own stores. He was a walking, talking promotion for his own brand, and he intended to keep doing it until he was 120.

CHAPTER FOUR

Gang

Get me a latte with a half-shot of butter rum. Make lunch reservations at the Hilton for Senator Smyth and myself. And see if marketing has the stats on those *Longevity Lozenges. Longevity Lozenges.* That name sucks—it's right out of the 50s. We need to get Whitman and his people to come up with a better name. And get me a flight to DC next Thursday morning, and a suite in the Mayflower for two nights. And where the hell are Sam and Carlton? They were supposed to be here 10 minutes ago."

Ida Morton had been Tyler Belknap's executive assistant for 15 years. Nothing seemed to rattle her. She could track with his long, Gatling-gun lists of demands and have them executed in minutes. She never let her emotions or opinions show on the job—unless Belknap made a sarcastic comment or one of his cheap, racy, politically incorrect jokes. Then a wry grin and a "ha" was in order. And, most importantly, she kept everything confidential.

Belknap lost his temper at least once a day—but never toward Ida. Not only was Ida his right hand, she was also his eyes and ears—plugged into a network of informants all over the organization. In a matter of minutes she could access useful information on any given employee, including who was doing what to whom. Ida was also adept at transmitting Belknap's impatience over the phone, which she could do with a simple "Dr. Belknap will see you *now*." It was all in the voice. The stone-cold voice. She commanded as much fear as Belknap himself—maybe more. If you weren't on her good side, you would never be on Belknap's. She was fiercely protective of him, his time and his schedule (perhaps a little *too* protective).

Carlton Vance and Sam Patrick were the exceptions to those in fear of Ida—mainly because they knew Belknap's real history. And Belknap was secure because he knew their history—a finely tuned system of checks and balances.

Vance entered Belknap's office without knocking, fully absorbed in a trade journal. The office featured a sweeping semi-circle of windows protruding from the building, commanding a 270-degree view of the Columbia River, Portland to the southwest and snow-capped Mt. Hood, about 80 miles to the east. His custom designed desk of inch-thick glass supported by wrought iron legs sat in the middle of the huge arc of windows to his back.

On the opposite wall hung a jaw-dropping juxtaposition of rather valuable paintings by Gustav Klimt (a later work), Georges Rouault and Paul Klee. In the center was a portrait of a decidedly robust and manly Jesus commissioned from photo-realistic western artist James Bama.

Chairs for guests formed a rough semicircle around the front of the desk, centered on Belknap. Vance plopped down in one of these chairs, still reading his journal.

"About time you showed up," growled Belknap, not looking up from his computer screen.

"Heck, I just heard about the meeting a half hour ago. What's up?"

"The farmers' co-op in North Dakota—the one that supplies our organic oats—wants to renegotiate their contract."

"First I've heard of it. That'll hurt us. The outfit in Ohio was the only one who came close to their bid and they were still out of the ballpark. Who's behind it?"

"Morgan, I think." Belknap was still preoccupied with his computer.

"You want me to send Richardson back there to see if he can dig up a little dirt—and then he can have a little talk with Morgan?"

"That usually works pretty well. I like Richardson. He's quiet, thorough and dangerous. He always comes up with something. Shoulda used him on you."

"Hey. That's uncalled for."

The door opened and Sam Patrick ambled in.

"Sam! Nice of you to make it to work this morning," snarked Belknap. "I was just telling Carlton here about our friend Morgan. But I think we'll be just fine, thank you."

"Richardson, eh?" Patrick grabbed a handful of Wellness 120 Organic Gumdrops out of a large obsidian jar on Belknap's desk, just as Ida popped in with Belknap's organic latte. She set it on his desk, but Belknap continued to focus on his computer.

"You're welcome," said Ida, dryly. "Can I get anything for you guys?"

"Sure, I'll have one of those," said Patrick, "and you got any of those cheese Danishes in the fridge?"

"I'll just have a bottle of mineral water, thanks," said Vance.

"Thanks," grunted Belknap, "Carlton, what are we doing about this whistleblower in our Phoenix institute—the one who says we hired an instructor even though we knew he'd had a problem in the past with underage girls?"

"I think we've nipped it in the bud. Turns out the whistleblower himself had an underage girlfriend when he was 18. We talked to the woman and convinced her that she should be willing to testify. Then we talked to the guy and he agreed to drop the whistle. Case closed."

"Was Bartlett involved in this?"

"Nope. He doesn't bother himself with HR issues— he lets me and HR take care of that. All he cares about is the academic side of things—and getting this guy trained internally so he can teach your... principles."

"What about the instructor?" asked Belknap. "Was it true?"

"Well, yeah."

"Okay. Let's transfer him to Kentucky. They've got a lower age of consent there, just in case. But tell him to knock it off and warn him that it better not happen again.

"Now—what about that accountant lady in our Oakland distribution center who was going around telling people I was full of beans. I heard she was amassing quite a little following for herself."

Belknap had endured his detractors over the years, both in and out of the organization. Over decades of sometimes bitter experience, he had learned efficient ways of dealing with both kinds of problems. Internal detractors were the most dangerous. Left untreated, they could cause internal rifts—attract followings and ultimately reduce productivity. Plus, they could leak internal issues to the media.

"That was a tough one," said Vance. "If we fired her she would just get more vocal and her little crowd would get even more upset. And she's smart, articulate and clean as freshly laundered money. I sent Richardson down there and he couldn't get anything on her. So we had our IT special project guy rig an embezzlement. Airtight and foolproof. He even made it show up in her bank account, as if it had been there for months."

Patrick spoke up, through a mouthful of gumdrops. "Our auditors discovered it yesterday and it's already been reported to the DA. She'll be totally discredited—end up in prison if we're lucky—where she can talk all she wants. Hey—we tried to work with her—warned her to settle down and mind her own business, but..."

"And we had a couple of follow-up sessions with the employees there—just to reinforce the idea that she was a serious flake," added Vance. "If anyone there has any more problems, we'll deal with 'em separately."

"Yeah, yeah—I'm always sorry we have to play these kinds of games—but we're doing the Lord's work here, dammit. We can't let people with a spirit of perversity obstruct us and gum up the works. Besides, what's an occasional life taken out of the way when so many people are having decades added to their lives?"

Vance and Patrick nodded in straight-faced agreement. No smirks. No eye rolling. They knew Belknap believed exactly what he said. "We gotta do what we gotta do," summarized Patrick.

"Any more customer problems I should know about?" asked Belknap.

"Our attorneys are working to settle with the five or six people we discussed last time. It's all good. They consented to non-disclosure agreements. Although a couple of them probably won't remember what they agreed to, but then they have no credibility. We have a new one in Pennsylvania who claims that our *Ante-*

diluvian Antacid capsules gave him an ulcer. We're working on that."

"Mm-hmm," Belknap nodded.

Ida brought in a tray with a latte, a mineral water and a cheese Danish. All organic. "Your lunch reservations with Senator Smyth are at 12:30, and remember your dinner at 6:00 with the gentleman from North Korea. Your travel arrangements for DC are on your screen. Whitman and his people will have *Longevity Lozenges* product identity options for you tomorrow, along with sales stats and demographics. The National Coalition for the Homeless is having a fundraiser next week at Waterfront Park in Portland. You may want to show up."

"Good! Thanks, Ida. Put that homeless thing on my schedule and let Dawson Criswell know so he can drop a word to the media."

"Thanks, Ida," chorused Vance and Patrick.

"Carlton," continued Belknap, "what about our little project? How's that going? I still want it in stores by this spring, you know."

"If you mean *Eternal Recall*, R and D still isn't getting consistent test results from lab animals. Sometimes it works, sometimes we get serious side effects. So at this point we can't say if it's going to be ready by spring."

"Well, they'd better get their rear in gear, because I'm not gonna back off on that rollout date. This could be the biggest thing for us since we started this business."

"But that would mean doing our human assessments before we work the bugs out. If something goes haywire, it could really bring on the heat."

"Then get busy and get rid of those bugs. This kind of thing is exactly the reason for my next topic."

"Which is?" asked Patrick.

"The many advantages of us of having a bigger presence in South America. The economy down there bounced back from the recession a whole lot quicker than it did in the US or Europe. We'll need to grease some palms in Buenos Aires to pull it off, but Sam can take care of that. They're poised for big growth—I mean big growth! I want you guys to fly down there next week and talk with our distributor. And let's think about a factory down there too."

"A factory? In Argentina?" queried Vance. "Why not Rio? Or São Paulo?"

"Because Brazil has laws in place regulating GMOs, and Argentina doesn't. Sure—Argentina isn't as politically stable and it seems to me that it's got more general business regulations, but on the other hand, I think they're more open to—*negotiation*. And as you know—we're doing some seriously cutting edge research lately with some very sensitive substances. It certainly doesn't hurt to have our eggs in several baskets. Even with my buddies in DC and Olympia, it's getting harder and harder to move the laws and regulations in our favor. There's more legislation on the Senate floor in Olympia right now about GMOs and labeling requirements—and it doesn't look good. Our freedoms to do the work of God are being eroded more and more every day."

"Maybe we should pray and fast," said Patrick, smirking.

"Great idea, Sam," said Belknap. "You can lead the charge by giving up those gumdrops, even though they're organic. I'm sure God will be so impressed that he'll make the legislation disappear right off of the Senators' laptops. In any case, we need to start laying groundwork in Buenos Aires now."

"You think the Board will go for it?" asked Patrick.

"Those old geezers will do whatever I tell 'em to."

"What about Bartlett?"

"Oh, Bartlett is never a problem. He's lost in his books and studies and in his deep, abiding faith." Sometimes you couldn't tell whether Belknap was being sarcastic. "Trust me. He's fine. His academic accomplishment, his contacts and his work for the Institute have given us more street cred than we could buy or steal anywhere."

"Yeah, yeah, I know, and he's highly respected in and out of the organization. But people like him bother me," said Patrick. "You always get the feeling that they're one or two steps ahead of you. That they know something you don't. It's like they're too—at peace or something. No anxieties or fears. Normal people have fears and you can use that to motivate them—to move them one way or the other. You can't get a handle on someone who's confident—who has no anxious thoughts. The other thing that bothers me about him is that I think he sees through us."

"Sam," said Belknap while entering a long line of text on his computer, "I have two comments about that. Firstly, what do you mean, 'see through us'? We have nothing to be ashamed of. Things that some may regard as shady or dishonest on our part are things we have had to do to further the work of God. We keep these things discreet because many would misunderstand. Secondly, as you very well know, I make it a practice *never* to let *anyone* get one or two steps ahead of me. If I hadn't been applying that rule in Los Angeles both of your tails would not have been saved."

"Yeah. Just remember who saved yours," snarked Sam.

Belknap gave a disdainful look over his reading glasses and grunted.

Vance was tracking a 767 as it flew behind Belknap's head on its final approach to Portland International Airport. "Yup. If we hadn't helped each other out, all three of us could be doing time right now in federal prison."

Belknap finished whatever he was writing, punched the enter key on his computer and rocked back in his chair with his fingers linked behind his head, flashing his big, cheesy grin, "Yes, my friends, we coulda been. And yet—here we are!"

———

If Tyler Belknap was an enigma, Clifford Bartlett was one just as much—except Bartlett's enigmatic quality derived from his depth. During WW2, Bartlett's grandfather had moved from Louisiana, along with thousands of other African Americans, to work in the Kaiser shipyards in Vancouver, turning out Liberty Ships. After the war, the Bartlett family moved to Portland, where Clifford grew up and earned his BA and MA at Portland State University. He had been looking for something worthwhile to do with his life ever since. In keeping with the city's ethos, he was a free spirit. He had worked variously as a researcher and fact checker for a local publisher, a writer for a Portland weekly and as a clerk in a health food store. He had even lived for a while in a rural commune in Estacada, southeast of Portland. But he preferred life in the city. He loved to browse the shelves at Powell Books while sipping coffee, and spent the rest of his time reading in his small northwest Portland studio apartment.

Bartlett had more than a passing interest in organic foods, health and alternative cures, so when Tyler Belknap appeared on the scene in the early 90s, Bartlett began following him. One day he decided to apply for a job in the newly opened Portland east-side Wellness

120 store on Hawthorne Boulevard. Bartlett's rich background knowledge of all things organic caught the interest of the manager, who mentioned him to Belknap. Belknap immediately pulled Bartlett into his headquarters staff to organize courses for the fledgling Wellness 120 Institute.

When Belknap opened an outlet in New York City, he sent Bartlett back to supervise the Institute—a perfect opportunity for the intellectually ravenous Bartlett to enroll in Columbia University's prestigious Mailman School of Public Health, where he earned a PhD in Environmental Health Sciences. Never tiring of academics, Bartlett went for a second PhD in Religion, by way of Columbia's cooperative arrangement with Union Theological Seminary.

Belknap was delighted to have Bartlett pursue these degrees, as they would be feathers in his organizational cap. After eight years in New York City, Bartlett had built a network of important connections—relationships that richly benefitted the company and gave it an air of legitimacy that Belknap could never have achieved on his own. Bartlett had more than earned his position as academic dean of the Wellness 120 Institute, and his seat on the board of the organization.

Somewhere in his religious studies, Bartlett had come to the conclusion that the traditional Jesus of organized religion seemed to differ markedly from the Jesus described in Scripture. The more he got to know the Scriptural Jesus, the more issues he began to have with Belknap and his organization. Up until then he had been like Whitman—cruising along, doing his job, aware that there were a few problems but not paying much attention and certainly having no thoughts about reform.

When Bartlett completed his Religion degree and

returned to Vancouver to work at Wellness 120 head-quarters, he was surprised to discover that there were several other Christian coworkers who were just as frustrated as he was. They talked and compared notes on Jesus, and on Belknap's rather strange spiritual universe. They hoped and prayed for change, but they weren't insisting on it. Belknap, after all, was Belknap.

Bartlett didn't owe allegiance to any church or religious organization per se—but he believed he knew and understood Jesus. And he was regularly in touch with many others who had similar feelings, in and out of church groups. Bartlett decided to stay on course, to do the best job he could, and to connect with employees who shared his perspective. But as he watched and listened, he began to suspect Belknap and his cronies of more than just off-beat religious ideas. Belknap spent too much time lobbying senators and congressmen. Employees were occasionally dismissed with no explanation. Secrecy surrounded certain departments, and the employees in those departments seemed to avoid eye contact. Something unethical or even illegal was afoot. Neither he nor his friends could pin it down yet, but he was certain there was something.

Sure, Wellness 120 products were good. Millions of customers swore by them. Maybe they were a little *too* good. Was Belknap doing something unethical, or even unsafe, to maintain his competitive edge? He was pretty sure Belknap had cut all kinds of covert deals with various government agencies—but was he enhancing his products, somehow? Increasingly, Bartlett had heard rumors of people suffering various ailments and blaming it on Wellness 120 products. A little of that might be expected with any big company—but these reports seemed to be more and more frequent.

Bartlett didn't want to be presumptuous. He wasn't exactly sure what action he would take if and when he found out more information about what Belknap was up to. Yet over time, he began to think beyond the immediate problems—to what a reformed Wellness 120 might look like, and how the reforms would be presented to and received by employees and the public.

Lisa Sanchez stirred white sugar and cream into her coffee, her eyes darting around the dining room at Nosey's Bakery. It was a Portland landmark—not the organic, sustainable, whole wheat kind of place that had become Portland *de rigueur* in the last decade—but the old-time bakery with sinfully creamy desserts, pies, cakes and rich pastries oozing with chocolate, butter and sugar. And outstanding Viennese roast coffee. No one in Belknap's organization who valued their job would be caught dead in such a place. That's why Clifford Bartlett regularly met here with various friends when they had matters to discuss relating to the sweeping reform he hoped would happen in the Belknap empire.

"There's something going on up there that I'm not comfortable with," said Sanchez finally.

"I don't doubt that," smirked Bartlett, across the table from her. "There's always something going on. Here's the real question: Is it something legal, moral and ethical, or is it not? Belknap and his friends have always made sure their operations appear squeaky clean. Every time we've suspected something out of order we've hit a wall."

"So far. But I think this time it's different."

"Okay. I believe you. How so?"

"Have you heard about *Eternal Recall*?"

"Can't say that I have," answered Bartlett, preparing again to be surprised by disturbing developments in the organization. "But I have a feeling you're about to enlighten me."

"It's a new product we're been working on for some time that's supposed to enhance memory. Belknap, of course, hopes it will be a cure for Alzheimer's. Its active ingredient is a particular chemical compound that occurs in some plants—most commonly found in *gymnocarpium dryopteris*."

"Ah, yes—the northern oak fern. I have several in my backyard. A tea prepared from certain parts of it was once used in folk medicine to cure melancholia—although there's some question as to whether this was true of the northern oak fern or its cousin, *polypodium vulgare*, the most common fern in this area. I use the young shoots in salads. Of course the oak fern dies out every winter, whereas *polypodium vulgare* does not."

Sanchez paused for a moment, always caught off guard by Bartlett's command of arcane information. "We've been manipulating the genes of this fern for a couple of years to increase the yield of the compound—dramatically."

"And—?"

"The compound has pronounced psychoactive properties, but no one else, so far as we know, has done any research on it. Just based on the studies we've done, we believe it may enhance memory in sufficient quantities—maybe—just maybe—even reverse signs and symptoms of moderate Alzheimer's. But the test results on our lab animals have been inconclusive. Sometimes they run mazes or learn new behaviors flawlessly. Other times they don't. And in a few cases they lapse into a coma. We're not sure whether that's a side-effect of the compound or some intervening variable."

"Interesting. And—?"

"This thing needs far more testing and rigorous

studies. As far as I'm concerned, it needs FDA approval. Of course Belknap doesn't care about any of that. He thinks he can bypass the FDA, because the product, as usual, will be made from natural, organically grown plants—not isolated chemical compounds."

"Right," agreed Bartlett. "*Gymnocarpium dryopteris* itself is not a controlled substance. As far as I know."

"But this strain should be, because it's been genetically modified."

"Hmm. I see. And of course it will be labeled as non-GMO."

"Yes. But that's not the immediate problem. The immediate problem is that Belknap wants to start selling products with this stuff in it next spring. That means we need to test it on humans this summer."

"And the 120 Institute Summer Program is coming up."

"You got it."

"Actually, I don't get it. If the product is intended primarily for a geriatric market, why aren't qualified senior volunteers being recruited for legitimate clinical studies?"

"My point exactly," said Sanchez, "but we aren't even to that place yet. About a month ago Belknap talked a couple of members of his Methuselah League into trying it. Thank God, they didn't have any trouble—and they both seemed to think their memories had improved, which is of course entirely subjective. Nevertheless, that's why Belknap feels so confident about moving ahead. Now he wants general testing on any human subjects. Even kids."

CHAPTER FIVE

Crossroads

"Hello, Dave. Clifford Bartlett here." Whitman always welcomed a phone conversation with Clifford (*never* Cliff—*always* Clifford). He invariably had a challenging insight or two, usually presented in a congenial way. He was able to put nearly any problem in context and perspective, simply by asking two or three questions. "Can we meet somewhere? Perhaps Nosey's Bakery in Portland. They have several wholesome organic selections on the menu."

Whitman agreed to be there in a half hour. Although he had been to Nosey's many a time he hadn't noticed anything remotely organic. Maybe Bartlett was pulling his leg, which he had a way of doing with a completely straight face—even over the phone.

When Whitman arrived he found Bartlett sitting in a booth back in a corner, drinking tea and enjoying, one small bite at a time, a large rum-fudge brownie. Dave tried unsuccessfully to mask his disbelief.

"Dave! Don't tell me you and Marcia haven't been here—because something tells me you have. Several times. I am assured this brownie and latte are completely, 100% organic, Dolphin friendly and sustainable to boot. May I order another for you?"

Whitman smirked. "Actually I prefer the cream-filled cinnamon rolls. And a cup of French roast."

"Aha! I thought I had you pegged as a dangerous subversive!"

Whitman pulled out a chair and sat down. A waiter took his order.

"Dave," began Bartlett, "I wish we could spend time chatting about things in general—but I need to get straight to the point. For reasons that will become clear as we talk, I feel that I need to take you into my confidence."

Whitman's curiosity was piqued, with some apprehension.

"I can tell that you are a clear and critical thinker," Bartlett continued, "and that you don't check your brains at the door when you come to work every morning. I also believe I can trust you to keep this conversation between us—and Marcia of course. May I ask you a couple of personal questions?

"Sure," nodded Whitman.

"Do you really believe Tyler Belknap has all the answers?"

Whitman was not surprised at this query coming from Bartlett. But his pulse quickened—he knew that a negative answer would be like opening a door from a cozy room where everything was neat and orderly, into a place of dissent, uncertainty and chaos. Ten years ago he simply would have gotten up and left the table—not necessarily out of loyalty to Belknap—but because to engage in such a discussion would have been a sure course to career suicide and social ostracization. But now...

"No, I don't." Whitman heard himself say. The door had opened. "I think he's probably well-intentioned, but his ideas and his organization have gotten a little out of hand." That was like opening the door a crack and peeking through.

"Okay. You are quite diplomatic, my friend. I might go a step further—and say that being 'well-intentioned' doesn't mean much. From what I've read, Hitler believed himself to be 'well-intentioned.' And I would say that Dr. Belknap's ideas from their inception have been beyond 'out of hand.' Just my opinion, but I believe they are dangerous and thoroughly unchristian."

Unchristian. Regardless of Whitman's increasing doubts and some of the information he was uncovering about Belknap, this seemed like a bold assertion— perhaps even a bit cruel. But Whitman continued to listen and keep an open mind.

"For instance, let's take his core idea—the idea on which all his other ideas and this very organization are founded—the 120-year human lifespan. In the context of the Genesis narrative, chapter 6, verse 3 could have two possible meanings. One—God was telling Noah that there were 120 years left until the flood. Two—God was reducing the lifespan of human beings from what it is said to have been in the previous chapters of Genesis. Given the context, the second explanation seems the more plausible of the two, especially since the narrative later informs us that human lifespans decrease. Moses lives 120 years, for example. But the text implies no *guarantee* of 120 years, even conditional on obedience, much less obedience to any 'wellness' or health principles. Further, those whose lifespans approach 120 today are often 'breaking' one or more of Belknap's principles of wellness. Not surprising, since the most recent research indicates that genetics plays an equal or greater role in longevity than environmental or behavioral factors.

"My point is that in light of both sound biblical

hermeneutics and empirical evidence, Belknap's assertion is untenable—and rather deceptive!"

Whitman had mixed emotions about where this
was going. In spite of his doubts, he felt okay with God
because he had been engaged in something "bigger
than himself" for the last 20 years. He was helping
people do the right thing, live longer and be healthier. Now Bartlett was sitting here across the table from
him, saying it had all been a big waste of time.

"When such erroneous ideas first sprout," Bartlett
continued, "they are regarded as innocuous little
seedlings, unusual, quirky. But as they mature, and
indeed these teachings have been maturing for some 20
years, they become cancer-like, monstrous organisms,
intent on consuming all in their path. Dr. Belknap's
teachings and tactics have now reached that point—like
some kind of GMO gone horribly awry. This has become,
both theologically and socially, a dangerous cult."

Whitman didn't entirely disagree—he *couldn't*
disagree—he had no arguments to counter what Bartlett
was saying. He tinkered with his spoon. The waiter
brought his French roast and cream-filled cinnamon
role. He ripped open a packet of sugar—white sugar—
and dumped it in his coffee, along with what he guessed
was non-organic cream from a small pitcher. He stirred
it and took a sip. "So, Clifford…how long have you felt
this way?"

"I will gladly share my personal journey with you
in time. But my concern right now is to know what
you are thinking behind that slick corporate façade."

"I…what façade?"

"Come now, my friend. You're quite adroit at masking your feelings, adopting a professional demeanor
and doing your job. And there's nothing wrong with that
in its context."

"Okay. So I don't totally buy into the stuff Belknap preaches. But nobody's perfect."

"Ha. There's imperfect and then there's deeply flawed. Dave, there's a group of us across the country. We've networked for years. Each of us had personal reasons for getting involved with Belknap—and each of us traveled a different spiritual journey in and out of the organization. But at some point each one of us recognized that Belknap's message isn't genuine Christianity—or that thing we call the *gospel*. This has nothing to do with it. For one thing, the real gospel is not a cash cow. And this organization is. It's that way because Belknap has always realized it's not enough to give people something to believe. They have to have something to *do*. Something to keep them busy. That's what keeps the revenue streams flowing.

"But I don't think it's the money that motivates Belknap," continued Bartlett, "or the power. I think it's the game. Unfortunately, that's the case even with a lot of Christian leaders. The game. Not Christ. Not service. Just the game keeps them going. They can never tolerate losing. They'll always find a way to keep playing.

"Think about it. Belknap's family is gone. His wife died over a decade ago. His kids have moved out of the country and don't talk to him any more. He has no close egalitarian relationships. People like Belknap can't have relationships unless they're in control. The three people closest to him are Ida Morton, Carlton Vance and Sam Patrick. Vance and Patrick were involved with him when he became shut out of the LA business community, and I'm not entirely sure about the precise nature of his relationship with Ida, but I think they are what we would call a "couple"—clandestine for about 10 years. He's still human of course, but in some respects he's lost much of his humanity. He's a business machine—and the most dangerous kind—someone who actually believes he's doing it all for God. And Dave, beyond that, don't think that the racial aspect is lost on me." Bartlett elicited a wry smile.

"What do you mean?"

"I mean, I understand that my academic degrees, my contacts and my seat on the board serve to make Belknap look magnanimous and progressive. *Wow. His organization must be cool. He's got a brother in a high position.* But how many African Americans does Belknap actually employ?"

"I don't know—not too many."

"Correct. That's what is commonly referred to as tokenism. Now, consider how many women are on the board or in senior management."

"Well, none, I guess."

"Right you are. None. Don't you see, Dave? Belknap only pretends to run a forward-thinking, enlightened company. In reality it's good-old-boy despotism."

"I don't get it. If you're on the board, why don't you just vote him and his gang out and hire new officers?"

"Two reasons. First, he has the board loaded with men who are unconditionally loyal to him, and second, the by-laws give him absolute authority to remove and appoint board members for no reason, at any time, without prior notice."

"Okay. That *does* seem autocratic. But is there anything illegal about it?"

"No. If the CEO and officers are ethical and responsible it should all work out just fine. If the CEO and officers are not, the door to corruption and abuse is open. That's why, in most corporations, the board has real power. Of course there are conditions under which we could appoint a new CEO and alter the by-laws—his resignation or incarceration to name two."

Dave was poking at his cinnamon roll with his fork. In light of his research into Belknap's background, he could feel himself easily conceding to everything Bartlett was saying. But what then? Would he start hanging out with Bartlett's group? And who else was in on this…movement or resistance or whatever it was? He could guess who the others might be, but then he never would have imagined that Bartlett would actually be involved in some organized subversive activity. And if he started hanging with them that would make him a subversive—a dissident. Was he ready for this? Was Marcia ready? How would it affect his kids?

"It's not that I object to people eating healthy food or taking care of themselves," Bartlett continued. "It's that we've made a religion out of it. And we've co-opted Scripture to build our case, which obscures the real gospel of grace—which has nothing to do with food, physical health or longevity. As the Apostle Paul says in Romans 14:17, '…the kingdom of God is not a matter of eating and drinking, but of righteousness, peace and joy in the Holy Spirit.' Yes, Jesus healed a few people and fed a few people. But it does not follow that his message was about health and nutrition. Physical health and longevity is commendable, and we'd all like ourselves and our loved ones to live long, healthy lives—but the Bible and the gospel are not about nutrition, health, medicine or longevity, any more than they're about zoology, botany, paleontology, genetics, geology or quantum physics! These disciplines are all part of the realm of human science—left for us to study using our God-given intellect.

"Belknap likes to sprinkle his speech and writing with Jesus and the Bible, but he knows very little about

Jesus. In reality he does that merely to appeal to the Christian market."

Whitman stared out the window, watching the Portland bicyclists dodge traffic and vice versa. "So you're telling me that for all these years you've been trying to get the goods on your boss. Isn't that disloyal? I mean, the guy has treated you so well. Don't you feel kind of…treacherous?"

Again, Bartlett smiled his wry smile. "Of course this situation is not easy or comfortable. But we're not so much trying to 'get the goods on him' as we are keeping our eyes and ears open—and being there when Belknap and his inner circle make a sizable mistake—so the damage can be minimized. I—*we*—believe the company is producing many good products and teaching a few good principles. Some products I'm not at all certain about. But we would like to see the foolishness and the religion stripped away and see the company reformed so it can effectively and responsibly do its job and make a positive contribution to society as a whole."

Finally, Whitman said, "Okay. I can see all that. But what would happen if we let things just run their course? I mean, Belknap may think he's going to live to be 120—but maybe he won't. The next guy may be more moderate. Stuff like this usually evens out."

"Two problems with that," answered Bartlett. "While on the one hand our customers may benefit from the healthy lifestyle—on the other hand there are all the rules, all the do's and don'ts, all the judgment, the religious legalism, the pandemic paranoia—that all takes a mental, physical and emotional toll on people. It's not ethical. It's using fear to increase sales."

"I suppose it is. What's the second thing?"

"The second thing is why I asked you to come here today. We have an immediate and pressing problem. I heard that your son has been selected to attend the Summer Institute." Whitman's thoughts about his own doubts and loyalty were suddenly on the back burner. The red flag in the Summer Institute release forms was suddenly looming large.

"Yeah—what about it?"

Bartlett told Whitman everything that had been reported to him by Lisa Sanchez. He told him about his initial concerns a few years ago when bits and pieces of information had started trickling in. But now he was reasonably certain. While everyone knew that Belknap liked to roll out a few new products at each camp— in recent years he had started using the kids as convenient guinea pigs for potentially dangerous new ingredients.

"Dangerous?" gasped Whitman. "What do you mean? You mean our products are laced with some kind of drugs or something? Isn't that a bit far-fetched?"

"Tell me, Dave—haven't you ever wondered why our products are so incredibly tasty—when similar products from our health food competitors have all the flavor of recycled cardboard? Why do some of our supplements make you feel so good? Not just good— *really, really* good."

"I don't know. Yes, I guess I *have* wondered—but it's not my department. It just doesn't seem possible that the people we work with would do something like this. I mean knowingly."

Bartlett sat back in his chair. "Well, maybe not knowingly. Maybe research, development and production is sufficiently compartmentalized that only a few know what's actually happening."

"Okay," said Whitman. "I suppose it's possible. And I guess that would explain the defensive tone of the consent forms for the Summer Institute. But at this point if we don't let Jason go, or start making up reasons why he can't, he'll immediately know something's up. And what about all the rest of the kids up there? There's really nothing we can do about this, is there? I mean all we have is Lisa's story, and if we confronted Vance or Belknap, they would deny it—and we would be fired, along with Lisa."

"Well, maybe there *is* something we can do about it, Dave. Here's a thought. Jason is a smart, reliable young man. What if you had a little talk with him and explained the situation? Do you think he would be willing to go in as sort of a mole—our agent—to help us discover the truth—perhaps even to gather evidence?"

This was all happening way too fast for Whitman. Now, suddenly, he was being forced to let Jason in on the possibility of some very sordid problems. Jason might not believe it, he might take it as a challenge, or he might become angry and disillusioned. But in any case, he would be better off knowing what might be going on than knowing nothing.

———⟫●⟪———

Dave and Marcia sat at the dining room table. Marcia's head was reeling from the all the information Dave had just dumped on her. "Do we have to do this?" Marcia asked, "isn't there another way? Can't we just call the police or something?"

"Call them and tell them *what*?"

"I don't know what to think," said Marcia. "I thought there were a few problems with the organization, but using kids as guinea pigs? I just can't believe it. Couldn't Bartlett be mistaken?"

Dave didn't say anything. Bartlett wasn't stupid—not one to jump to conclusions. He was a respected board member, with two PhDs. He just didn't make judgment errors of this size. Then on the other hand there was Belknap and his inner circle. Dave had worked for them for two decades. They were businessmen—aggressive and ambitious, and Belknap was a brilliant showman. But that's what it took to be successful. They had always treated him decently. He'd heard stories once in a while about people who claimed they had been harassed and threatened—but he had written them off. Maybe he shouldn't have.

"You know—maybe it's all overblown," said Marcia. "Maybe they're just trying out a few new products or snacks to see how the kids like them. They do that all the time anyway. And someone got the wrong idea and got all upset about it and complained to Bartlett."

Dave sat for a while. "Well—unfortunately I think there's a lot more to it than that. As much as we want to avoid throwing cold water on Jason's summer, we need to talk to him. Yes—I hate to see him disillusioned and burdened with stuff like this. But at some point he's got to come face to face with the grim world we live in."

The Wellness 120 Institute Summer Program was underway. Students had been trickling in all day and most of them were familiarizing themselves with the surroundings, meeting up with their friends and checking out the opposite sex.

The evening of arrival was marked by a gala reception, with live music provided by one of Portland's premier Christian rock bands. Over a hundred students and at least that many staff milled, chatted and noshed on healthful concoctions. Uniformed waiters roamed among the students and staff, offering champagne glasses filled with sparkling organic cider from the organization's own apple orchards in the Yakima Valley. As the waiters cordially encouraged them, students, faculty and other guests began moving toward the Conference Center auditorium.

Out of the west, there came the thumping of a helicopter—growing steadily louder and finally appearing over the trees. Students who were still outside gaped as the 5-seat Eurocopter EC120B Colibri touched down on the nearby helipad. It was bright metallic green with a huge 120 lettered in white on each side. With a 17,000-foot ceiling and a 440-mile range, this quiet, efficient machine was perfectly suited for trips to Belknap's farms and properties in Oregon and Washington, as well as entertaining politicians and suppliers with trips to the coast or remote areas of the cascades. With the rotor still moving, Belknap opened the door and energetically hopped out, ducking and waving at the same time. Applause from the young people was sudden and thunderous, punctuated by the whistles and hoots you might expect from high school kids. Almost unnoticed, Ida Morton, Carlton Vance and Sam Patrick disembarked behind Belknap.

Waiters again motioned for the remaining kids to enter the auditorium. Inside, Belknap mounted the stage and the thunderous applause and shouts continued. Belknap didn't motion for it to stop, either—he seemed to pause for a long 30 seconds, absorbing the accolades. Finally he motioned with his hands, and the group fell silent. Belknap, knowing how to create drama, let the silence run for a full 45 seconds as he gazed at his group, pointing and grinning at a few kids he had met personally. Even if the event had ended right there, everyone would have gone back to their cabins thoroughly inspired.

Belknap began: "Twenty five years ago, I was rockin' a Porsche 928. Livin' in Bel Air. Big mansion. Tons of money. Then—suddenly I was broke. Nothing. No job.

Nobody was hiring. On top of that I was feeling bad all the time. The only thing I could do was move up here and put up a trailer on my brother-in-law's farm in Brush Prairie, just a few miles from here. All of a sudden, instead of a new Porsche I was driving an old John Deere tractor. I thought I would be driving that thing for the rest of my life."

A thunderous chorus of laughter broke out. Belknap really hadn't said anything funny, but the incongruity of Belknap, who had just arrived in his own helicopter, driving a tractor seemed humorous to this group.

"Nothing wrong with driving a tractor—that's good, honest work. But God quickly showed me that he had more urgent things for me to do. Things that would bring health and happiness to millions—things that have already added a total of thousands of years to human lives."

More assent from the audience.

"Those were tough days for my family and me, but as I dug into God's word day and night—by the light of an old kerosene lantern in our trailer, because we couldn't afford electricity—God's plan for me became totally clear. And now—25 years later—that has become God's plan for all of you!" Belknap made an expansive, sweeping gesture.

"The thing is, you guys don't have to go through what I did. You're all here now. And in the next four weeks you're not just going to have a blast—you're going to find out what you need to know to still be having a blast a hundred years from now! I mean that! Look—all of you want to live a long time—but you don't want to be old. Well, I'm telling you that you don't have to get old—you can just live! If you just follow a few rules."

"How many of you have read my first book?" About

a quarter of the hands went up. "Hey—I appreciate that, but I know somebody's lying because I sure wouldn't have read my book at your age."

Uncomfortable laughter from the group.

"Why would I? There's too much other stuff to do! But that's not a problem because right here at this camp you're going to discover all the stuff in my book while you do the stuff you want to do. And it doesn't cost you a thing! What kind of a deal is that, huh?"

Applause and cheers. The kids were starting to relax. It seemed that even though Belknap was well over 40 years their senior, he had the ability to charm them—or any audience for that matter.

Several of Belknap's Methuselah League turned out to mingle with the kids and show them what they could expect if they strictly obeyed *The Eleven Principles of Wellness*. Belknap, as usual, was delighted with the evening's activities. But he didn't stay too late, because he had other, pressing business.

As Academic Dean of the Wellness 120 Institute, one might assume that Bartlett was involved in every aspect of the Summer Institute. Not so. Leaving the details to those who were gifted with the skills he lacked had never been a problem for Bartlett. Years earlier he had hammered out a syllabus for the class component of the camp, and he had reviewed the course outlines for the physical and recreational activities, but those things were not Bartlett's forté. There were plenty of other employees with experience in those areas.

Bartlett personally taught the orientation classes—and he always enjoyed leading groups of kids on hikes through the forest, teaching them to identify edible plants in preparation for survival week.

But this year was different for Bartlett. With the disturbing information that had come to him recently, he was having trouble viewing the camp as anything more than a cage full of hapless guinea pigs.

Carlton Vance was in charge of the camp. A committee of department heads reported directly to him, but he had compartmentalized certain departments to maintain confidentiality. The recreational staff had little information about what the medical staff was doing with their myriad tests; the food staff had little or no idea what the R & D people were up to. It was generally understood that a few new products were market tested every year at camp to see what that age group thought. Only the Research and Development staff, Carlton Vance, and Tyler Belknap knew the extent of the tests and what was really being tested. In an office, hidden not far away in an abandoned silver mine, R and D chief Steve Capell knew what each student was eating, as well as his or her vital signs, blood composition and mental acuity. With the exception of an RN and a phlebotomy technician, the medical staff had no medical training. They were researchers whose normal jobs were back in the abandoned mine. Each summer, instead of working with white rats—they worked with young humans.

CHAPTER SIX

Survival

Jason shared a cottage with four other guys, two from the east coast, one from the south and another from California. He felt good about this because he was acting as sort of a Pacific Northwest host for his new friends. That, his stature, his athletic prowess, his positive energy and generally likable personality (plus the fact that his dad worked for Belknap) made Jason a natural leader of the group in his cottage.

Jason's parents had filled him in on the possibility of unpredictable ingredients in the food and supplements before he left for camp. He was still absorbing what they had told him. Sure—he had agreed to watch for anything that seemed unusual—and to avoid supplements or unidentifiable foods. The plan was that he would discreetly slip supplements into his pocket and stash them in the hidden compartment in his backpack. Then he would turn them over them to his parents when he got back home, and his dad would turn them over to somebody else for analysis. Of course, Jason wouldn't tell anyone else about it. But he had trouble taking this too seriously. He really didn't think they would find anything unusual. Why would anyone do something like that? And up here with new friends and the prospect of all kinds of sports and challenging activities, his parents' cautions seemed remote. He would be on the lookout for anything unusual— but he felt safe enough.

The first two days at camp were spent alternating between informal discussion groups (which were really orientation classes) and a few physical activities. Then a whirlwind of woodland activities started— sports, hiking, fishing, swimming, water skiing, kayaking, archery and marksmanship. A steady stream of vans shuttled groups of kids and staff around to different venues for activities that were not supported at the Retreat Center.

Everyone was looking forward, some with trepidation, to the survival skills section. This would be reserved for the last week of the session, as the kids would need every bit of the skills they had learned earlier.

The food, of course, was outstanding. A large part of Belknap's success in the marketplace was due to the fact that his healthy food products actually tasted good. Not just good. *Really, really* good. Competitors had tried to reproduce his recipes, but had failed so far. Part of the appeal of this camp was the food. Healthful *and* tasty pizza, fries and burgers. Cola that seemed to taste better than the "real thing," and seemed to have a bigger caffeine/sugar buzz, even though it was allegedly caffeine-free, refined-sugar-free and made with only natural, organic ingredients. Even the salads and veggies tasted better.

The first thing Jason (and everyone) noticed was the *way* the food was served. No cafeteria lines. No waiting. You used a smartphone app to make your choices (smartphones were available on loan for those few who didn't bring one), and your meal was delivered to your table on a tray. Trading food was strictly forbidden, they said, because part of the purpose of camp was to keep each student on a strict, individual-ized dietary regimen, to achieve maximum health ben-efits by the end of camp (or at least until they went off their diets for the survival section). The medical and kitchen staff had plenty of information on everyone's allergies and food preferences. There were supplements, of course. Each packet of pills came with a little printout explaining what they were and how they would help you. No one paid much attention. But Jason noticed that the pills looked a little different for each student. Most of the time he just slipped them in his pocket and put them in his secret stash back in the dorm. But sometimes he did-n't bother. He just gulped them down like everyone else.

The next thing Jason noticed was the frequency of medical tests. Campers' vital signs were monitored dai-ly. They were weighed, measured, EKG'd and stress tested every three or four days, with slightly less fre-quent blood draws and urine samples. Then there were the mental acuity games—which seemed more like tests to Jason. Nothing seemed devious about this—they were told upfront that their health and fitness was being monitored, and that they and their parents or guardians would get to see just how much they had improved by the end of camp.

<hr>

About two weeks into camp, Jason found himself riding a horse. Not like it was time for the equestrian section, and so he went to the stables with a bunch of other kids, saddled up and got on a horse. No. He just found himself riding a horse. It was as if he had just awakened—with no recollection of how he got there, what he was doing before, or what he'd done for the last day or so. He looked around. He was part of a string of 10 or so kids on horseback, riding up a trail in the woods. He had no idea where. He felt panic begin to well up, and then got control of it. *Okay,* he thought, *we're riding single file. I don't have to talk to anyone, so I'll just relax and enjoy the ride while I try to get my brain back.* After about a mile, bits and pieces begin to filter in. Then whole chunks of memory. Finally he remembered getting up this morning, having breakfast and walking down to the stables. And here he was. By the time they got to the end of the trail on the top of Larch Mountain, he had recovered his memory and everything was normal.

Jason didn't share his experience with anyone. He just chalked it up to the fact that he had been up until 3 that morning with the other guys in his cottage playing video games on their smartphones. And it certainly couldn't have anything to do with what his parents were talking about. *It's just that I'm not a kid anymore. I need my sleep,* he told himself.

A couple of days later, Jason was doing archery. He had just drawn an 80-pound recurve longbow and was taking aim when suddenly a stream of impossibly vivid images flooded into his head, apparently from when he was an infant. Eating in a high chair. Lying on a changing table. Crawling around on the floor. Playing with his teddy bear.

The arrow not only missed the target but also veered off at a 45-degree angle, narrowly clearing one of the female students standing on the sidelines.

An instructor rushed over to Jason. "What the heck was that? Are you crazy?"

Jason looked pale. "Sorry. I...I think I'm okay. I guess my fingers slipped or something."

The instructor stared at him. Jason's fingers never slipped. He was one of the best natural archers the camp had ever seen. "Alright. You don't look too good. Maybe you better go take a rest."

"Nah—I think I just let myself get a little dehydrated." Jason grabbed a bottle of water and drank the whole thing.

That night at dinner, Jason asked if anyone occasionally had flashbacks from when they were a baby. "Um, I think, like I have this memory of like being in a doctor's office?" answered one guy across the table. "And I remember him poking me with this needle? I think he was doing a blood test or something. That's really all I can think of. The rest of my memories are a lot later—like riding my tricycle or playing with the dog and stuff."

Beyond that, Jason didn't tell anyone. He figured the flashback—if you could call it that—was just a temporary glitch.

—————⟫●⟪—————

Camp was in its second week. Vance and Patrick were in Argentina on business that superseded their other responsibilities. The timing was not perfect, but Belknap felt that he had to act now. He'd seen dissent in his organization a couple of times before, and he had always dealt effectively with it. But it was never quite as stealthy as this. It had to be nipped in the bud. There were numerous tools at his disposal. There was the tactic Vance had used with that lady in the Oakland distribution center—which at once took her out of circulation and discredited her among her following. But in this case, Belknap didn't know who the dissidents were. He knew only that more than one of Ida's sources had told her there were people waiting in the wings—waiting for Belknap's "chickens to come home to roost." This of course ticked him off. Beyond that, he found it disturbing that anyone had knowledge of any "chickens." Or did they?

In any case, the appropriate action would be to

smoke out the Troublemakers by engaging and galvanizing the bulk of the employees who were loyal to him—arousing their suspicions about enemies in their midst. And even if no real opposition or threats existed, periodic witch-hunts were always excellent devices to draw the rank-and-file together, circle the wagons and get their minds off other problems.

All Belknap needed to do to start the ball rolling was to call a quick employee meeting of everyone at headquarters, and maybe the managers of his local plants, local stores and local institutes. He didn't need to bother anyone at the Summer Institute. They would find out quickly enough.

—————⟫●⟪—————

The corporate elite of Wellness 120—the headquarters staff—filed into the small auditorium in the basement of their office building. It wasn't as spacious as the one at the Retreat Center, but it was big enough to hold all the employees in the building plus a few more. Whitman had already found a seat when Bartlett sat down beside him.

"Do you know what this is about?" asked Whitman.

"No. Not a clue," Bartlett replied. "I saw Jason a few days ago. He looked happy and energetic. Asked a couple of good questions in my Basic Physiology class."

"Hmm. Good. Maybe the trouble you expected won't happen after all."

"Dave—I really hope there won't be any trouble."

Suddenly Belknap took the stage and strode to the lectern. He was not grinning. He was wearing a somber, matter-of-fact look, like a President of the United States about to announce the bombing of some foreign enemy's capital city. The group greeted him with vigorous applause, which was normal when Belknap spoke. He motioned for quiet.

"You know, any meeting like this should be a joyous occasion—God's headquarters leadership and workers here together in one accord. Friends, just look around you. This is what God has accomplished through you and me. Every day, through our products and our teaching we are proclaiming His plan of health and prosperity for all humankind. Lives are being changed. People are living longer and healthier!"

The audience nodded and murmured in agreement.

"But my friends, I'm deeply sorry—*deeply* sorry—to have to tell you that there are some few right here among us—possibly even today in this very auditorium—who do not see it that way."

The audience fell silent and sober. Heads turned slowly. Eyes glanced furtively.

"These few do not agree with the leadership God has provided and ordained for his work! They have a different vision. Like Korah in the wilderness with Moses, they are intent on doing things their OWN way. When you listen to these people, what they are saying may *seem* right. But as Proverbs 14:12 tells us, 'There is a way that seems right to a man—but in the end it leads to death.' Friends—be on your guard. Rumors and wild stories are being spread. When you hear this kind of idle talk, I need you to do two things for me.

First, I need for you to consider—*prayerfully* consider *on your knees*—would these fine and godly people tolerate and condone such things as are being murmured about?"

At that cue, the eight members of the Methuselah League, walked onto the stage behind Dr. Belknap. The audience again erupted in applause, and rose to its feet. Dr. Belknap stood aside as the applause continued, then returned to the lectern and motioned for silence.

Of course, Whitman and Bartlett rose to their feet and applauded enthusiastically along with everyone else. Whitman's blood pressure had risen about 10 or 20 points. He was not used to being included with the enemy. Yet here he was, standing right next to the ringleader! He wondered if people were watching him. Suddenly he was aware of his body language and his expression. Was it right? To make matters worse, Bartlett leaned over to his ear and muttered: "Brilliant! Masterful move!" Whitman stared straight ahead, as the group sat down again.

"The second thing I need you to do for me," continued Belknap, "is if you hear any of these rumors, just give my office a call. That's right—Ida will be expecting a few extra calls this week. Let her know what you know. Friends, the last thing we want is trouble, or to have to see someone lose their job. And that's why we want to nip this thing in the bud right now—and to get these people the help they really need and get them back on the right track. We just want to continue to do God's work—and God knows there's a lot to be done! Now how about it—are you with me?"

Again, thunderous applause and cheers exploded. This time it seemed to go on forever. In less than 10 minutes Belknap had effectively crushed any rebels within his organization. Or so he thought.

Again, Bartlett leaned over to Whitman, "This is exactly what we thought he'd do." Again, Whitman stared straight ahead and continued clapping. But when he finally turned toward Bartlett, he was amazed to see Bartlett moving down the aisle toward Belknap, walking right up to him and shaking his hand.

"Good to see you Clifford, my friend," said Belknap. "I really hate having to do something like this, but we can't risk having splits and schisms in the organization—especially when we don't know who or where they are."

"Oh, I understand completely sir," said Bartlett, "and this is clearly the most effective tactic. A brilliant move. But tell me, do you know the source of your information? Because if it's coming from anywhere in the Institute, I want to do everything I can to sort it out."

"Thanks, Clifford. Good. I figured you would do as much. I've always been able to rely on you to get things done thoroughly. Ida Morton heard this third-hand, so it's hard to track down. But apparently it's not localized in one area. It's scattered around the country. And these people aren't really doing anything that you can put your finger on. Just waiting. Waiting for what, I don't know. And talking to each other. It's the darn-dest thing."

"Hmm. Well, I guess I'll just keep my ear to the ground and let you know."

"I can't tell you how much I appreciate that, Clifford." Belknap patted him on the back, grinning again. "We've gotten through everything else. We'll get through this."

Don't count on it, thought Bartlett.

Whitman was standing at the side of the auditorium, taking it all in. Bartlett turned, walked up the aisle, greeting people along the way, and joined him.

"I can't believe you did that," said Whitman, just above a whisper.

"I had to see if he really knew anything. He doesn't. He just knows that people are out there who disagree with him."

In a minute they were outside the building in the parking lot where they could talk more freely.

"Don't you feel hypocritical? I mean trying to cover up your real feelings like that? Looking him square in the eye? Pretending to be what you're not?"

"You mean prevaricating? I'd be prevaricating if I told you it wasn't difficult. But at some point I suppose one has to decide whom one is serving. Am I serving Belknap or am I serving a higher Authority? Am I serving an inanimate corporate entity or am I serving its flesh-and-blood employees and customers? Sure—it'd be a whole lot easier and far less complicated and duplicitous to tell Belknap exactly what I think and resign. But would that move the organization toward genuine reform? As a board member I've come to see that we have a greater responsibility to the people we serve—and really to Jesus himself."

Bartlett could see he was pushing Whitman's envelope. "I know. It's all pretty heavy stuff. But talk it over with Marcia. Give it some thought. I think you'll understand what you need to do."

Whitman said nothing, but inwardly conceded that Bartlett was right.

———————————

The time had come for the great survival week. It was not a whole week—only five days—but it might seem like a week for those who were unprepared (or if the weather turned damp). The fledgling survivalists' return to civilization would be followed by the final end-of-camp celebration. Jason and 15 others were backpacking up a remote trail about two miles east of the Retreat Center. Teams of three kids would be dropped off at various points in the forest. It was not as though they were going into the wilderness entirely unequipped. Each student had a sleeping bag, basic cooking implements, three energy bars, a first-aid kit, a couple of bottles of water, a knife, a roll of twine, a small hatchet, a tarp, a change of socks and underwear, and a solar rechargeable smartphone with geolocation and topographic maps.

They would need to improvise their own shelter, start their own fire without matches or lighters, and find their own food. The smartphone offered safety and security against getting lost, and enabled staff (camped nearby) to know their precise location. Hunger would motivate them not to waste a lot of time Skyping, texting or playing games.

They had received training in useful aspects of survival—recognition of edible and non-edible vegetation, how to craft small weapons or fishing tackle if they wanted to catch birds or fish (for those students with appropriate licenses). Catching and eating rodents was discouraged, and larger game was highly improbable and illegal with no hunting tags.

Jason, Evan and Liam separated from the rest of the group, accompanied by an experienced staff member. He would guide them a mile or so up into the forest. After that they were on their own.

It took them a while, but they discovered a south-facing rocky outcrop that would hold some heat from the sun and serve as one wall for their shelter. Jason immediately set to work finding a vine maple tree, as its branches could be used to make a bow and arrows. Evan looked for branches to build a decent lean-to. Liam looked for salmonberries, huckleberries and vegetables that could be cooked—such as agoseris, arrowhead, beargrass, burdock root or bracken fiddleheads.

By late afternoon they had a shelter, a campsite, a couple of pheasants roasting on a fire, a pot of assorted wild vegetation boiling and a bag of wild huckleberries for dessert. They had worked so hard in the afternoon building their camp and searching for food that they were out cold as soon as they hit the sleeping bags.

———————

Dave and Marcia Whitman were feeling more

uneasy all the time. They lay awake at night wondering if they had made the right decision in letting Jason go to camp. The situation prompted them to dig deeper into Belknap's background. They spent hours online every evening looking for anyone Belknap had worked with in the 80s in the big LA media company where he claimed to have been so successful. Finally they found a couple of people who remembered Belknap. As Dave and Marcia suspected, the company Belknap worked for wasn't as big as he had portrayed in his book. Yet Belknap had actually worked on a variety of accounts—everything from car manufacturers to breakfast cereals. His favorite client, however, was Reverend Horner Bagley, a successful southern televangelist who wanted to be taken seriously—a tall order for any publicist, ad agency or media specialist. It seemed that Belknap had learned all about the big business of institutional religion from Reverend Bagley

Just about this time, the Whitmans concluded, Belknap was probably beginning to think of striking out on his own. They imagined at this point that Belknap would be pondering two big factors: 1) strategy and 2) capital. Belknap may have considered becoming a televangelist or something like that, yet religion of and by itself seemed iffy. He could develop a message and write a book. Then after a few years of hyping and pushing that message, it would get stale and he would need to reinvent it—to find ways of restating it—to find fresh ways of engaging the fickle public. It seemed that Belknap concluded the best approach for him, given his skills and expertise, would be to combine some type of product with religion—to make people think that God would be more pleased with them if they consumed a particular product—to use religion as an incentive to drive sales.

Capital was another problem. Here's where the Whitmans had to do some intense sleuthing. Marcia contacted an HR employee of Belknap's media company who had kept floppy disks formatted for the old CP/M operating system, with a list of employees from 1986. She borrowed the disk and found someone with a functioning 64k Televidio computer. From the list she found a woman who had worked in the accounting department. The woman turned out to be a wealth of information. She told the story of Carlton Vance and Sam Patrick, who had been skimming funds off their heavily padded expense accounts for years. When Vance became CFO of the company, he continued to do so on a much grander scale. Sam Patrick, as chief accountant, facilitated the process. A couple of employees suspected something was amiss, but were reluctant to blow the whistle.

According to this source, Patrick, Vance and Belknap were notorious drinking buddies. The Whitmans surmised that Belknap had become aware of what his friends were up to, perhaps hiring geeks to hack into the company's financial records and extract enough evidence to get Patrick and Vance in big trouble. He made them an offer they couldn't refuse. That's where, over a period of months and years, Belknap acquired the capital to launch his own new enterprise. At some point, he must have offered Vance and Patrick positions in his future endeavor, since he needed their unprincipled skills. Vance and Patrick, of course would reciprocate by protecting Belknap.

Had Belknap already planned the narrative he would later include in his book? Possibly. In any case, the financial markets cooperated. A recession hit. The company, already weakened by embezzlement and other crooked dealings, began to tank. Belknap arranged for himself to be among the first casualties. Pretending to be destitute, he moved with his family to semi-rural Southwest Washington and set his new scheme in motion, later calling for his cronies to join him.

It was an incredible story of intrigue and an unprincipled man who later seemed to sincerely believe everything he was teaching. But the best flim-flam men often end up believing the very deceptions they have concocted.

The Whitmans didn't know exactly what to do with this shocking information. So they kept it under their hats for the time being. But Dave intended to share it with Bartlett the next day. The next day, however, would present other distractions.

———➤●◄———

Pitch dark. Why? Why am I standing here in the dark? It smells like woods. Am I in the woods? How did I get here? I can see stars through the trees. And the sky looks a little brighter over there. But I can't see my feet. I can barely see my hands. Why am I here? Who am I?

Jason didn't remember getting up in the middle of the night to take a leak. The campfire was out so he took his flashlight and walked through the trees only a few yards away from the campsite. He had just turned around to go back when the continuity of his memory ceased. Initially, he knew nothing. After two or three minutes of standing there, he remembered his name, then his family. Beyond that, nothing. Certainly nothing about camp, school, college, friends, and nothing about his earlier memory "glitches." He focused on the immediate problem.

I can't move without light. What do I have in my pockets? There it is. A small LED flashlight! What else? Some coins. A pocketknife—good. That's it? Wait. Some kind of snack bar. I don't feel hungry so I'll keep it. Why am I in the woods at night without a backpack or sup-

plies? A cell phone. Why don't I have a cell phone?

He had left his cell phone, his billfold and everything else back at the campsite—but of course he remembered nothing of those things or the campsite. Now he needed to start moving. But which way? Jason scanned the area with his flashlight, looking for anything that might suggest where he had come from. A building— a car—a tent—a footpath. There was nothing visible. But not more than 10 yards away, obscured by the dense understory, was the small shelter with Evan and Liam snoozing quietly. Then Jason made a decision.

If I head downhill, I might find a stream that I can follow—maybe for miles. But if I go uphill, by daylight I might find a vantage point to look for a house or a road or smoke from a campfire. I'm heading uphill.

Had Jason chosen to go downhill, he would have encountered the campsite and his friends. Uphill, unfortunately, was nothing but a long trek to the top of a broad forested ridge with no good vantage points.

After an hour of struggling uphill through the tangled understory of fern, vine maple and an occasional painful berry vine, Jason entered what seemed to be a small clearing. His flashlight picked up yellow metallic glints in the moss and soil. He dug at one with his finger and pulled out what appeared to be a 30-millimeter shell casing—and another—and another. They were all around.

A few steps away, another large piece of metal half protruded from the soil. He reached over to grab it— but suddenly pulled back. He didn't know how, but he recognized it as the top portion of a land mine. Maybe he had read about it somewhere or seen one on TV.

Is this left over from some huge battle? Where is this place? Am I even in America? America. Okay. I know I'm an American.

Jason had no idea he was walking through an old army firing range, and that he was traveling in a direction that the guide had warned him against the previous day—an area where there might be old unexploded ordnance left over from Camp Bonneville.

Jason moved back among the trees, concluding that the clearing might hold more dangerous surprises. After another 15 minutes of struggling through the underbrush—still moving uphill—he heard a rustle off to his right and quickly aimed the flashlight in its direction. Two gold eyes reflected back at him, perfectly still for a moment, and then disappeared into the darkness. A brief crackling of twigs suggested that whatever the eyes belonged to was not small. His pulse quickened.

His flashlight was not as bright as when he started. He was tired, and his memory had not improved one bit. He was discouraged and starting to panic. Somewhere through the dark forest Jason became aware of the sound of rushing water. He was thirsty, but the last thing he wanted was to fall into a stream. He would explore in the light of morning. He sat down with his back to a huge Douglas fir. He prayed—not really knowing what to pray for—other than help.

When he awoke, birds were chirping, sunlight was filtering through the trees and a jet contrail was directly overhead. *At least I know there's civilization somewhere*, he thought. He also thought he heard an engine of a small plane in the distance—but not close enough to do him any good. The worst part was that his memory was the same. He remembered his father, mother, sister and grandparents—but little else. At least the panic was gone. And he remembered the snack bar in his pocket.

Hmm. Wellness 120 Energy Bar. I wonder what that's all about?

As he was taking a bite of the incredibly delicious bar, he again became aware of his thirst and of the sound of nearby water. He was also aware of something new—the smell of smoke. Several yards through the underbrush brought him to a stream. The water looked clear so he stooped to scoop up a drink of the cold liquid with cupped hands. Further up the hill he could spot a series of little waterfalls, but the relatively flat terrain of the clearing made the stream slow down and form a small pond.

A rustling in the bushes at the edge of the pond caught Jason's eye. Leaning over to see past the vegetation, he was shocked to see a man fishing. Before Jason could pull back to decide what to do next, the man turned toward Jason and waved, almost as if he expected him to be there. Hope and relief welled up. Jason made his way through the ferns and blackberry vines. Now he could see the source of the smoke he had smelled earlier. A few feet behind the man on the shore a campfire burned with fish roasting over it. A weathered backpack lay on the ground with a knife, a tin plate and eating utensils.

The stranger was dressed in jeans, hiking boots and a well-worn, heavy canvas jacket. His complexion was swarthy, and Jason imagined that he might be Middle Eastern. He had longish black hair and a short beard. His friendly face was scarred and pockmarked, as though he had endured a terrible case of acne when he was younger, Jason surmised.

"How you doin'?" asked the man, intently watching the point where his fishing line entered the water.

"Um—not too good right now. I think I'm lost. And I don't remember...um..."

"Don't remember what?" Ripples radiated from the line and the tip of the pole jerked down a couple of times. The man yanked up on the pole, and reeled in a 12-inch brown trout. *How do I know this is brown trout?* thought Jason. The man extracted the hook and line from the fish and laid it on a rock next to the fire.

"I don't remember anything," said Jason. "I don't know what I'm doing here, or who my friends are, or..."

"Hey," said the man, "It's gonna be okay. Your friends aren't that far away. They just started looking for you a few minutes ago. It'll probably take them a while to find you, but they will find you. So just relax. Look, Jason—I found you didn't I?"

"Yeah, I guess you—wait—how do you know my name?"

CHAPTER SEVEN

Search

After a day of backpacking, setting up camp, hunting and gathering, Evan and Liam had no problem sleeping—not even on the ground in their primitive shelter. It was well after daybreak before Evan's eyes blinked open to the sounds of the awakening forest and the sound of a small plane flying overhead. Liam was still snoring away, but Jason's sleeping bag was empty. *Typical,* thought Evan. *Jason is the guy who's always up first and on top of things. Where does he get all his energy?*

Evan poked his head out of the shelter, expecting to see a campfire and breakfast already cooking—but the campfire had gone out and everything looked the same as they had left it the night before. Maybe Jason had gone hunting. He looked back at Jason's sleeping bag. His cell phone and other gear were still there. He pulled on his clothes and shoes and walked around the camp, peering through the trees. Nothing.

"Hey, Liam! Get up. Help me figure out what's goin' on here."

Liam was equally baffled, but not worried. "He's probably off stalking a moose or something."

"I dunno," said Evan. "His knife and bow and his other stuff are all here. I think we oughta have a look around. Just in case he did something stupid or got eaten by a cougar."

They gathered a few essentials, including water and a few energy bars, and set out in widening circles around the camp. The third time around they spotted a footprint, headed uphill. They moved in that direction. Sure enough, they were able to trace Jason's movement by a trail of broken ferns, bent vine maple and an occasional footprint. They didn't report Jason's absence to the staff on their cell phones because they thought for sure they would find him around the next tree, aiming at a pheasant with a newly fashioned vine maple bow.

But after about an hour and a half, they lost his trail. Admitting defeat, they called for help.

<hr/>

"Jason, my friend. It's good to see you. Why don't you sit down on this log for a few minutes and we'll talk." The stranger picked up the two sticks that skewered the fish roasting over the fire. "You know, you're going to be out here for a little while longer. You just polished off that energy bar, but I think you need a more substantial breakfast. How about some fresh trout and fried potatoes?"

Still unsure, Jason watched as the man used a fork to deskewer the two fish onto a tin plate from his backpack. A small pan full of crispy potatoes sat on a rock by the fire, having obviously been cooked earlier. The man dumped the skillet into the plate with the fish.

"I know you love fish, and personally, I think there's nothing like fish broiled over a wood fire for breakfast. I think you'll really like this—I've served up a lot of fish."

Jason reached out and took the plate. "I *am* hungry. This looks great! I love fish! Thank you." Jason tentatively sat down on the mossy log. It was funny. He didn't recognize the man but he felt like he knew him, or had known him well at one time in the past, whatever his past might have been. For some reason, Jason felt comfortable and secure. Somehow he knew that this man would tell him the truth.

"I've got something important I want you to do for me," said the stranger. "I'll tell you right up front it won't be easy. But you've always responded to challenges."

"What do you mean?" asked Jason through a mouthful of trout.

"Well, for one thing, the plans you made about college and a medical career—I'm afraid a lot of that will change."

"Okay—whatever you say—but I don't remember making any plans—or anything. Do I know you?" Jason strained to remember. It seemed like he'd known this man for a long time. He had a familiar face and a manner that made Jason feel comfortable and made any vestiges of his earlier panic melt away.

"Here's the thing, Jason. Your memory is going to be a big challenge for you for a quite a while. You'll have trouble remembering a lot of things and people. But you won't forget this conversation, and in time it'll all make sense.

"Your father's boss has caused a lot of grief, so I'm creating a situation where he'll be out of the picture. Eventually I'll deal with him and he'll come to his senses, but that's no concern of yours. This man has been using you, your friends and a lot of others—to experiment with some very unstable chemicals in the food and supplements he sells. He'll stop at nothing to beat his competition, and to circumvent any laws that get in his way. He's tampering with things he doesn't remotely understand, and your memory loss is a result of that. Beyond this, he's giving people the wrong idea about me. Of course there's all kinds of religious teachers and institutions out there doing that—and I'll take care of all of them in time—but I'm taking care of this one now."

Jason was gaping, trying to absorb what he was hearing. "I don't understand any of what you're saying—I don't have any point of reference. Why are you telling me all this?"

"The chemicals he has given you have affected your memory in radical ways that he and his researchers didn't expect. I'm afraid parts of your memory have been seriously damaged. Jason, you know I could repair those problems, don't you?"

"What—are you some kind of doctor?"

The stranger laughed. "You might say that. My point is that if your memory damage remains for the time being, the man who has done these things will be forced to leave and let my friends take charge of his organization. They'll transform it into something good and helpful. That's what I do, Jason. I transform things that are evil into things that are good. I find things that are lost."

"Well—I guess I'm lost."

"Actually, Jason, you're not," laughed the stranger. "I know where you are. At any given time I know your exact location."

Jason thought this man seemed to know an impossible amount of stuff about everything. It was dawning on Jason who this might be, but of course that was crazy. *But then*, thought Jason, *in my condition how can I know what's crazy and what isn't?*

"You're not crazy," smiled the stranger. "You're going to be up here in the woods for a few more hours.

Then after they find you, you'll spend some time in a clinic and then in a hospital while they figure out what caused your condition. You'll have your family and a lot of good friends around you. But here's the tough part—your memory just won't be the same as it was. Do you understand?"

"Yeah—this all sounds kind of scary."

"I know. But by going through this, you're going to help and encourage a lot of people—millions of people. Eventually you'll be responsible for changing some major laws, and saving people from things that are even worse than what you're going through. Are you with me?"

"I don't know. I guess if it helps a lot of people and I'm the only guy who can do this…"

"And remember, as you go through all these experiences, I'm there for you and your family."

"What did you say your name was?"

"Just call me Josh."

<hr />

Carlton Vance was taking a nap in his huge tufted leather office chair, his feet propped up on his eight-foot-wide, 28-thousand-dollar, custom-crafted rosewood desk. He did this just about every morning at 10:00, unless there was a meeting or unless Belknap had some large bee in his bonnet. Carlton was dreaming about Buenos Aires—sitting on his veranda while a servant brought him a Caipirinha. Just as he was taking the first sip, he was startled by a loud jangling. What could it be? There was no phone on the veranda. No, wait—it was the real-life phone on his desk. Annoyed, he answered it.

"Carlton Vance here. Uh-huh. Uh huh. Oh for crying out loud. Lost?! Can't the little bastards find their way around in a few trees? We give 'em cell phones, for Pete's sake. We teach 'em how to catch food and how to build a shelter. What the hell is wrong with 'em? Okay. Okay. Yeah, I know. Who is it anyway?"

Vance's expression rapidly changed. His face paled slightly. He sat up and lowered his feet to the floor. "Oh no…no…dammit. That's Dave Whitman's boy. Yes, our Creative Director. What are we doing so far? Okay. Okay. I don't care. Do more and do it now. I'll be up there in a few. Call me if anything changes."

Vance cradled his head in his hands for a few seconds. Then he got up, grabbed his coat and headed down the hall to Belknap's office. But he had momentarily forgotten—Belknap wasn't in—he was in DC taking care of political business. Vance asked Ida to call ahead to flight operations, where there was always a pilot on the ready. In less than five minutes, Vance was seated in the metallic green Eurocopter Colibri, streaking through the air northeast toward the Retreat Center.

<hr>

Jason had parted ways with the stranger who called himself Josh a couple of hours ago. He wondered why Josh didn't just lead him out of the woods. But then Jason couldn't remember what was outside of the woods. Jason knew he had family but had no idea where they were. Maybe this forest was where he lived, or maybe he lived thousands of miles away. Josh had not actually clarified any of this. He had said something about friends and something about his dad's employment. It was odd. He could remember every detail of his conversation with Josh, and his energy had been more than restored by the meal Josh had prepared for him. But he still couldn't recall anything more than his family and his own name. Now, after he had left Josh, he thought of a hundred questions he could have asked.

In any case, Josh had suggested to Jason that he should keep moving uphill. So he did. He was searching for some kind of ridge, rock or vantage point so he could spot any signs of nearby civilization.

He arrived at what appeared to be a long outcrop of igneous basalt at the top of the hill. One lofty outcrop towered over the 150-foot Douglas firs—more than enough for him to reconnoiter in all directions. Jason began climbing the outcrop. It looked at first like an impossible climb, but he was surprised to find himself intuitively selecting footholds and handholds and making his way up the sheer wall of basalt.

How do I know how to do this, and why aren't I more scared of heights?

Finally he made it to the top. By then the sun was nearly overhead. Judging from where it had risen, Jason inferred his compass points. Not surprisingly, he was surrounded by heavily forested hills...to the southeast, a huge, snow-capped peak dominated the horizon— apparently a stratovolcano. To the north another snowy mountain loomed. This one looked like its top was missing, probably lost in some huge cataclysm in the distant past. Much further to the north was another large mountain with two summits. Yet another jutted up to the northeast beyond long ranges of rugged hills. In the distance, to the west-southwest, Jason saw a flat hazy patch that could be a city. He could see tiny specks moving through the haze that he guessed were aircraft, perhaps flying in and out of an airport. Glimmers of reflected light suggested that a large river or lake lay between him and the city.

Okay. So there's civilization way out there. That's good to know but it doesn't help me now. I need to find something a lot closer—a road—a house—a building— anything.

Jason looked southeast again. The hill he was on fell away into a deep ravine. Across the ravine was another hill with an escarpment about halfway up that looked like it might be a road. He sat down on a rock and watched for a truck or an SUV. After about 15 minutes, he wondered if it would be worth climbing down the ridge, crossing the ravine and climbing up the other hill to the road. What if it wasn't a road? What if it was just a trail? What if no one came by? Still, there was a greater chance of meeting someone on the road than up here on this rock.

From the west there came a steady thumping, gradually increasing in volume. It startled him at first because he couldn't associate the sound with anything. Remembering the spent rounds of ammunition he had discovered on the way up here, he wondered if it were some fearsome, large-caliber machine gun—like the 30mm chain gun on an AH-64 Apache attack helicopter.

Wait. Where did that come from? How do I know that? And that's what that noise is—a helicopter! But what if it is a gunship? If I'm in some kind of war zone, how do I know whose side they're on? How do I know what side I'm on? Maybe they're not hostile—maybe they're looking for me. Should I stand up or should I hide? Josh didn't tell me anything about this. I don't know what to do!

He squinted into the distance, straining to see something—and then he saw a speck, moving low over the hills, but getting larger. It was definitely headed this way. Jason decided to lay low until he could see if it was a gunship or something more benign.

––––––>●<––––––

While they were still half a mile from the Retreat Facility, Vance spoke to his pilot through his microphone. "Hey, Norm—can we swing around over that hill where the Whitman kid disappeared? I'd like to get a feel for the terrain up there. Probably can't see a thing through the forest but it's worth it just to get a basic idea."

Norm reduced his airspeed and veered to the left. About a mile east of the Retreat Facility, they spotted a congregation of vehicles on a dirt road. Twenty-five or 30 people were scattered around, some huddled in groups. A couple of German Shepherds hopped out of a Clark County Sheriff's SUV. Norm slowly turned his craft toward the top of the hill, no more than 50 feet above the treetops. It was hard to see much of the forest floor, but they caught a glimpse of a campsite—perhaps the one where Jason and his friends had been the night before. At the top of the ridge there was a large outcrop of basalt. They cleared the ridge to the north of the outcrop and circled to the south. "There!" shouted Vance. A figure was clinging to the east side of the outcrop, as if trying to hide from the helicopter that had been approaching from the west.

———

From his vantage point, Jason had been watching the helicopter. He watched as it lost altitude and disappeared just below the brow of the hill below him to the west. Then he watched as it rose from the trees and slowly climbed the hill veering just to the north of his rocky outcrop. As it neared, he could see that it didn't look much like a gunship, but how could he know? Maybe a sharpshooter was sitting in the door, waiting to pick him off. But why? He couldn't be sure about anything. He clambered backwards down the east side of the rock to keep himself out of sight. But by then the helicopter had crossed the ridge to the north of him and was circling south. Suddenly, it slowed and began to hover about 100 yards away. It was too late. They had spotted him. He could do nothing but cling to the rock and wait for the inevitable searing pain as the bullets hit his back.

Instead, he heard a loudspeaker calling his name.

"Jason! It's okay! Climb to the top of the rock and stay low. We'll land and pick you up there!"

"Do you think you can land this thing in that little space?" Vance asked Norm.

"We'll give it a try. It's just the updraft from this side of the hill..."

Norm eased his craft over toward the rock. As Jason tried to pull himself up, the downdraft from the rotor hit him. His foot slipped and he lost a handhold. Suddenly he was slipping down the wall. About five feet below, his feet hit a shelf. The rock above him was smooth with no footholds or handholds. He was stuck.

<hr/>

Dave, Marcia and Brandi Whitman rolled their car to a dusty halt behind several other vehicles parked along the dry mountain road. They could see a helicopter hovering at the top of the hill to the east of them. It was some consolation to know the company was sparing no expense to find their son. However, Dave had not heard the news of Jason's disappearance from any official source. Parker Stevens, a friend who was working in the Summer Institute, had called him earlier that day with the shocking news. Dave lost no time in picking up his family and heading east toward the mountains. "It just doesn't make sense," he told Marcia on the way up, "Jason is an experienced outdoorsman. He hunts, fishes, climbs rocks and knows every mountain, hill and creek in this forest. How could he just up and get lost? He doesn't do stuff like that."

"What about the stuff that Clifford told you? What about all the sleaze we discovered about Belknap and his gang?" Marcia had asked. "You don't think this has anything to do with them testing stuff on those kids, do you?"

"I don't know what to believe anymore," Dave had said.

"Will they find Jason? I'm worried about him. What if he tangled with a bear?" Brandi had asked.

"It's gonna be okay Brandi," Dave had answered. "They'll find Jason and he'll be fine."

———⟫●⟪———

Inside the helicopter, Vance and Norm could see Jason's predicament. Vance quickly rummaged through the emergency packages behind the back seat—pulling out a large coil of rope. A Coast Guard veteran, he quickly tied it to bracket with a clove hitch, opened the door and fed the rope down to Jason. Ignoring the 300-foot drop below him, Jason reached out twice before successfully grabbing the rope. He instinctively wrapped it around him, securing it with a Yosemite bowline knot. *How do I know how to do this?* Jason thought.

Above, Vance further secured the rope and gave Norm a signal to pull the ship up. Slowly, Jason walked up the wall, holding on to the rope. When he was back on level rock again, Norm slowly dropped his craft down until it rested at a slight angle on a relatively smooth piece of basalt. Jason was standing about 30 feet away looking unsure.

Vance, still in his grey business suit, jumped out of the craft and walked over to him.

"Jason! Good job. Thought we'd lost you for a minute there. We've been looking for you for hours. What are you doing way up here?"

"I...I don't know. I don't know anything. Who are you and why are you after me?"

Uh-oh, thought Vance. *We may have a problem.* "Jason—you know me—I'm your dad's boss. It's okay. You're at the 120 Summer Institute. Just come with me and get in the helicopter and we'll take care of you. Don't worry."

Jason remembered what Josh had told him, and he didn't trust this man who had just hopped out of a helicopter any further than he could throw him. But here he was, stuck on top of a rock with no way to escape. He decided he had better appear to cooperate, at least. Hesitantly, he climbed into the helicopter. Only then did Vance get a good look at the confusion in his eyes. "Do you know where you are, Jason?"

"I guess I'm in the woods somewhere. I don't know why. I woke up last night and I was just standing in the woods in the dark. Tried to find someone but no one came except for some guy in a canvas jacket, who gave me a plate of grilled trout and fried potatoes."

Vance stared at Jason. *He's hallucinating. Oh, crap. This is probably the product testing—maybe that* Eternal Recall *stuff that Belknap insisted on testing. I can't let anyone see this. My gosh—what if this is happening to the other campers? Got to keep this under wraps for the time being. In the meantime, I can put the best possible spin on it.*

"Jason—in a minute we're going to land on the road where everyone is starting to search for you. Don't worry and don't say anything. Let me do all the talking, okay? I just want you to stay in the helicopter—and then we'll fly you down to the clinic to have you checked over. Okay?"

"Sure. I guess. Whatever."

Norm set the Eurocopter down in a small clearing

next to the road where all the cars and people were congregated. Everyone stopped what they were doing and stared to see who would emerge. Carlton Vance stepped out and motioned for the group to come closer.

"I have really great news," Vance began. "Our crisis is over. Less than an hour ago, when I was informed of Jason's plight, the first thing I did was drop to my knees in prayer. And now we have an answer. You may have seen our helicopter fly overhead. Just a few minutes ago our pilot, Norm Waters, and I found Jason Whitman at the top of this ridge. He appears to be in good condition, he's here in the helicopter right now, and we'll be flying him down to a private clinic to be checked over." A big cheer went up from the crowd. People peered at the helicopter to see if they could catch a glimpse of Jason.

Unknown to Vance, Jason's parents and sister were in the crowd. When they heard Vance's news, they ran over to the helicopter to greet Jason. Of course, Jason popped out. The crowd gasped. Vance turned, looking a little surprised and slightly concerned. Jason hugged his mom, dad and little sister.

Vance continued. "As you can see, Jason is fine. We just want to get him thoroughly checked over by doctors to make sure everything is alright. On behalf of the family and Dr. Belknap, I want to deeply thank everyone for turning out here in short order to help search for Jason."

Meanwhile, Jason was talking with his family, and was also visibly disturbed. Jason looked perplexed. "I don't understand any of this. Why was I lost and why did I have to be rescued? I have no idea how I got out there in the woods in the first place. I don't remember anything!" Jason's voice was loud enough that the group, including any reporters who were present, could hear everything he was saying.

As Vance finished his comments, he noticed Jason talking with his parents. Things were getting out of control very rapidly, and he needed to rein them back in. "Marcia, Dave, Brandi—good to see you. Folks, we have to get this young man down to the clinic to make sure he's okay. Jason, if you'll just get back in the aircraft. Norm, ready to depart?"

But Jason was not ready. "I want my family with me or I'm not going."

Vance looked grim. Now the family knew about Jason's memory problem. There was no way he could suppress that anyway. And perhaps this flight would be a chance to reassure the family that the company would be only too happy to provide medical care to diagnose and treat Jason's mysterious problem. "Okay Jason. Okay. Pile in everyone."

The Eurocopter lifted up, cleared the tall trees and headed westward, back to the city.

CHAPTER EIGHT

Homecoming

Only a few people knew about the Wellness Clinic. Belknap had established it for himself, members of his immediate family, his board members and members of his Methuselah league. Housed in an unmarked building in an upscale business park, it was separate from the headquarters complex, so that no one would ask questions. Belknap had furnished his clinic with the most up-to-date equipment and staffed it with a full-time general practitioner, a physician assistant and as many nurses as were needed, depending on who was in there. Specialists could be called in at a moment's notice. The roof was equipped with a heliport.

Aides immediately installed Jason in one of three luxuriously appointed guest rooms. Dave, Marcia and Brandi waited in a cozy lobby while doctors examined Jason. Two burly security men sat playing cards at a table in the corner. Dave thought this seemed a bit pretentious for a medical clinic, but was thankful for the attention being given his son. On the short flight and limo trip here, Jason had clearly recognized his family, but seemed to be completely unaware of his situation, or of what state, county and city he was in. He knew nothing of camp, of Wellness 120, of his school or his aspirations. He seemed to have a few facts, but they were without context.

After about a half-hour the general practitioner emerged along with Vance. They were talking in muted tones. Then he walked over to the family and introduced himself.

"I'm Dr. Waycroft. Your son seems to have experienced a rather catastrophic loss of much of his long-term memory. His sensory, short-term and procedural memory seem to be working, as he has relatively comprehensive recall of events since sometime last night, and he was able to make rational decisions and assessments as he attempted to navigate through the forest. Judging from what his friends have reported, he must have gotten up to relieve himself and experienced the event while he was in the woods, a short distance away from the camp. Since he didn't remember the camp, he simply couldn't find his way back, and instead proceeded up the hill. We suspect some ischemic event, similar to a stroke, but we'll need to do CT scans to confirm that."

"What's the prognosis?" asked Marcia. "How long do you think this will go on?"

"We really have no way of knowing, since this is all rather unusual. We'll know more when we see the scans tomorrow. Oh, yes—there's one more thing. He claims to have met a man in the forest who provided him with a meal of broiled trout and fried potatoes. Since this is virtually impossible, we conclude that he must have been hallucinating at some point, or that this is merely a misplaced memory fragment."

⟞●⟝

Belknap didn't like cell phones that much. He kept one on his person, but rarely answered it, letting texts and voicemails accumulate and getting back to callers at his own convenience, or more often than not, turning it over to Ida and letting her sort it all out. Not too many people had his number—Ida, of course, Vance and Patrick—his kids (who never called him anyway)—a couple of other board members and a few of his top security personnel.

That morning Belknap had hosted a breakfast for a few members of the House Agriculture Committee. As much as he schmoozed them, he felt that progress was increasingly difficult. GMO laws were getting more restrictive all the time. Belknap was so discouraged that he had to drop into the bar at the Mayflower Hotel where he was staying, only a few blocks away from the White House. He was sitting at a table in a dark corner, nursing a double shot of Laphroaig Scotch—a whisky with a flavor so strong that surely it must contain some kind of redeeming nutrients. *Hmm. I wonder if we could market a line of organic Scotch whiskies,* Belknap mused. *Holy distilled spirits. 120 proof.*

Belknap's cell phone rang. This time, he answered. It was Vance, calling from the Wellness Clinic to fill him in on the day's events. "My gosh," exclaimed Belknap after listening to the story, "can't I leave you in charge without all hell breaking loose? We've got to keep this quiet, and we've gotta make sure everyone who knows about it understands that this was some kind of pre-existing condition or stroke or something like that, okay?"

"I know—and I'm trying to keep it under wraps."

"Any of the other kids up there having problems like this?" asked Belknap.

"That was one of my first questions for Steve Capell. Apparently there are five or six other kids who have been a little confused. A couple of them got up in the morning and couldn't remember where they were for a while. And others just became disoriented."

"Hell, I've done that more than a few times myself," answered Belknap. "But they were nothing like the Whitman kid, I hope."

"No. Nothing like the situation with the Whitman kid. And the staff managed to keep a lid on it, so the other campers wouldn't start to freak out."

"Okay. Fine. Is Waycroft onboard? Make sure he knows what we have to do!" Belknap demanded.

"Absolutely. He's already been working on Dave and Marcia. I'm pretty sure they're buying it," said Vance.

———————

While Marcia and Brandi visited with Jason in his room, Dave went out into the parking lot and called Bartlett. Bartlett had already heard the story from a couple of reliable sources, yet when he compared Whitman's version, a few important details were conspicuously missing. The first was the mysterious stranger Jason said he had met in the woods. The other was the extent and nature of Jason's memory loss.

"Frankly, Dave, what you're telling me is not consistent what I know of strokes and other ischemic events such as aneurisms. Jason has had no history of anything like this. His physicals have shown no predisposition for atherosclerosis, am I correct?"

"No," said Dave, "but things like this can happen. My uncle Herb had a massive stroke with no warning at all and he was only 43."

"Dave—Jason is not 43. He's only 17. I know this is difficult, but I'm afraid we have to face the most likely cause of this."

Whitman felt anger rising within him, and at the same time a profound despair. The whole thing was still so hard to believe. Well, at least if it was some kind of substance the effects would wear off, wouldn't they? Or would they? There was no way of knowing right now—and if this was the result of some test, Waycroft and the people in the clinic were likely in on it. The new information on Belknap's early years that he and Marcia had just unearthed didn't do anything to assuage Whitman's growing paranoia.

And by the way, it occurred to him that he hadn't shared that new information with Bartlett yet. Whitman told him the story.

"Well, that explains a lot," said Bartlett. "But it doesn't change our immediate problem.

We need to find evidence of the substance Jason has ingested. Did he save any of the supplements they gave him?"

"I don't know for sure. We talked about it. He said he was going to stash them in a secret compartment in his backpack. His stuff is still up there, and camp is still in session, so I'll have to go get it."

Bartlett paused. "Hmm. Even if we retrieve those supplements, we have no way of knowing if that's everything they gave him. Of course, the supplements he kept may not be the same as whatever he ingested. They could have added some of it to his food. I wonder if there's a workstation in the kitchen where they assemble all this stuff. There has to be. The problem is, of course, that they are likely testing different products or substances on different people."

"Wait. Are you suggesting that we sneak into the kitchen at night or something and find the storage area for these supplements or—whatever they are? Do we even know what to look for? They're probably inside a locked storage room in locked cabinets with coded names. It would be a fool's errand."

"I know. It may seem foolhardy, but if indeed Jason has been given some substance to bring about his condition, then the most direct way for us to confirm that, and the best legal evidence, would be for us to locate a container of those materials labeled with his name. Our first task is to look for something like that. Yes, they may be protected and coded, but then again they may not be. As far as security is concerned, I'm Academic Dean of the camp and you're the corporate Creative Director. Chances are that no one will question our presence there—and likely none of the workers are even aware that any dangerous substances are part of the campers' daily supplement regimen, since everyone operates on a 'need-to-know' basis."

Whitman considered. "Won't people think we're snooping around or something—after Jason's 'accident'?"

"I don't think so. Yes, your son was lost in the woods. The staff up there will know that he was lost and was found. I guarantee you no one knows why, except maybe for Lisa Sanchez, her boss Steve Capell and a few other people in R and D. And of course Vance, Waycroft and maybe one or two of his associates. Criswell has almost certainly issued an internal statement and an external press release designed to cover it all up."

"Okay," conceded Whitman. "You're probably right. And I guess we don't have a choice, do we? What do we do?"

"We have to act fast," said Bartlett. "We'll visit the kitchen right now—today! I'll pick you up in 10 minutes and we'll drive up to the Retreat Center."

Whitman called his wife, who was still in Jason's room. "Don't look concerned. I'm going up to the Retreat Center with Bartlett to get to the bottom of this. If anyone asks, tell them I'm relieved and happy that Jason is safe and being given the best of care—but that I had to go pick up Jason's belongings."

<hr />

By the time Bartlett and Whitman walked in the door of the Retreat Center dining room, it was four in the afternoon. They had already picked up Jason's personal items from his dorm, including what he had taken with him into the woods. Whitman had quickly unzipped the hidden compartment and felt around. Sure enough, there were a couple of handfuls of capsules in there—but they needed more.

With the students still in the woods practicing their survival skills, the Retreat Center was nearly empty except for staff, preparing for the students' return in a few days. Bartlett and Whitman poured cups of organic coffee and sat down at a table. No one paid any attention.

"Probably the most rational thing to do is for us to go back to the kitchen and start up a conversation with someone and distract the staff with some kind of question. While I do that, you can look around," said Bartlett.

"Aw gee, Clifford. This is just too stupid. We're going to get caught for sure."

"Don't worry. I've got you covered."

Bartlett led the way back to the kitchen. Immediately he spotted Diane Rogers, assistant chef. "Ahh! Just the person I was looking for!" effused Bartlett. "I need your advice! I'm having a dinner party in a couple of days. I want to serve veal with artichokes and I wondered what kind of wine you recommend using in the recipe."

"Hmm," considered Diane. "You must be thinking of veal picatta or Marsala. I usually don't use wine to make veal with artichokes."

Another cook chimed in. "I've used Sherry—with excellent results." "Sweet or dry?" asked Bartlett. Within seconds most of the kitchen staff was crowded around Bartlett, offering their opinion or listening.

Whitman backed away and sampled a melon ball from a large caldron. He noticed an open door to a room with large filing cabinets. He slipped inside. One cabinet was clearly marked "Student Supplements." Each of four drawers contained a quarter of the alphabet.

"W" was in the bottom drawer. *This is absurdly easy,* he thought. He opened the bottom drawer. It was filled with thick folders, each one labeled with a student's name. There it was: "Jason Whitman." He pulled it out.

Inside the folder was a compartmentalized plastic container with each compartment labeled with a date. Most compartments were empty, except for the remaining days of camp after the students returned from their survival expeditions. It was all quite clear. What wasn't clear to Whitman was how he was going carry the folder out of here. On top of the file cabinets were some large manila envelopes. He slipped the folder in one. Then as an afterthought he picked up a felt-tip pen and wrote in large block letters "KALE KOOKIE CONCEPTS."

Whitman emerged from the room and joined the veal mini-conference in progress. Bartlett glanced at Whitman and noticed the large Manila folder under his arm. "Diane, this has been enormously instructive. Thank you—all of you! I know you have to get back to preparing dinner. I'll let you know how the veal with artichokes goes. And really, I need to do this every time I have a dinner party. What a vast wealth of culinary knowledge is contained within these walls!"

The staff looked very pleased with themselves. As Bartlett and Whitman turned to go, Diane, whose regular job with Wellness 120 was in product development, noticed the envelope. "Kale Kookies? What on earth is that? Can I see?"

Whitman tried to fake a genial chuckle. "Sorry. It's one of those top-secret projects that one of our marketing guys came up with. Doesn't sound too palatable now, but when we get all the promotion and packaging together, it'll be flying off the shelves. Oh yeah—I guess you guys'll have to come up with something halfway edible to put in the package."

Bartlett laughed out loud. Diane and the staff chuckled nervously at Whitman's mild cynicism. The two men headed out the door and back to the parking lot with their evidence in hand. Whitman was still suffering from an acute case of denial. He still had difficulty believing that these supplements contained anything more than the benign vitamins and minerals he supposed were in most Wellness 120 products. Yes, his son was in trouble. But it was hard for him to believe that Jason was the victim of a conspiracy.

They were just about to get into their cars when Whitman spotted R and D chief Steve Capell walking quickly along the other side of the parking lot. He slipped through a gate and into the forest.

Whitman waited for him to reappear. "Did you see that? I wonder what's going on there."

Bartlett was curious as well. Capell's office and staff was in the headquarters building. But he had heard talk of another R and D facility. Bartlett had paid little attention, since the company had so many different facilities for agriculture, manufacturing and distribution. And because of its competitive nature, R and D was generally kept out of the public eye. But here was the head of R and D disappearing into the woods. What did it mean?

"Let's go take a look," said Bartlett. "There may be security cameras trained on us right now, but what's the worst they can do to us?"

Bartlett and Whitman walked to the other side of the parking lot. A six-foot cyclone fence surrounded it. Capell had disappeared through a rolling gate protected by a card-key lock. Thinking he had nothing to lose, Bartlett tried his key in the lock. Surprisingly, the gate opened.

"Maybe it's because I'm a board member and I have a high level of security clearance. I don't know." They walked around the rocky outcrop and up a well-maintained road. After a while they were in an increasingly narrow canyon with a stream flowing far below them—apparently the same one that flowed through the Retreat Center. Eventually, they came to a massive iron security gate. On one side of the gate was a sheer drop of about 50 feet down to the stream. On the other side was an equally high wall of basalt. Only the most intrepid rock climber could find a way around. This time Bartlett's card key wouldn't work. Instead, a voice emerged from the cardkey device. "Can I help you?"

"Yes, this is Clifford Bartlett. I'm with Dave Whitman. We were just stretching our legs—exploring this little trail that led from the parking lot—and wondered where it went."

"Yes sir, Dr. Bartlett. The trail dead-ends just a few yards beyond this gate—blocked by a landslide a couple of weeks ago. It's pretty dangerous, and we're working on it. We installed the gate to make sure no one gets hurt."

"Okay. Now we know. Sorry to bother you. Thanks for the help!"

"No problem. You have a good evening, Dr. Bartlett, and you too, Mr. Whitman. Glad to hear your son made it back to civilization."

"Thanks," answered Whitman. "We're glad to have him back."

Clearly, something up the trail was off limits to the public, campers, employees and apparently even key executives. It was something neither of them knew anything about despite their years of service and positions. And as a board member, Bartlett shared in the responsibility for whatever was going on there. As they headed down the trail, Bartlett, said only one word in a grim, cynical sort of way: "Fascinating."

Suddenly, Whitman felt far less trusting of the organization—not only the leadership, but also the regular workers. These were people he thought had been his friends for decades. He knew the voice on the other end of the intercom. It was Jon Fulbright. His son was a couple of years younger than Jason. How could Jon lie like that? Whitman had seen Capell disappear up the trail with his own eyes. Something was going on up there—something they were trying to cover up. Who could Whitman trust?

As they walked in silence, Bartlett could sense Whitman's increased anger and confusion. "Thoughts?"

Whitman shot a glance at Bartlett. "Right now I don't know who to trust. I don't even know if I trust you. But I guess I have to."

Back in town, Bartlett and Whitman paid a visit to an old friend of Bartlett's at the Washington State University campus in Salmon Creek, just north of Vancouver. Tracy Horton was an expert in genetics and molecular biology, as part of the WSU Agricultural Sciences department. Bartlett took an hour to explain the background and what they suspected was going on— that Belknap may have been testing GMO foods and supplements on students at his summer camp, and that some of these foods and supplements may have been genetically modified to contain powerful psychoactive substances, and these substances might be responsible for Jason's condition.

Tracy sighed and glared at the pile of capsules and pills the men had retrieved. "There's a lot of stuff here. This is going to take a few days. Fortunately I've got several grad students and I can work these tests into their schedules."

Bartlett and Whitman were disappointed. They

hoped to have some more-or-less concrete evidence that they could take to the Washington State authorities or even the FDA so they could strike while the iron was hot. This meant more time for Belknap and his research staff to cover their tracks. In the meantime, Jason was in Belknap's clinic. Of course Whitman could decide to take Jason home or to take him to the family doctor, who of course would refer him to a specialist. It's not like Jason was physically impaired—he had simply lost his long-term memory, except for his family, and even that was a little shaky.

Bartlett drove Whitman back to his house to pick up his car. By then it was 8:00 pm. "I know you're worried about Jason there in the clinic. We know they're almost certainly prevaricating as to the cause of Jason's memory loss. We can also be reasonably certain they won't experiment with other substances to counteract what he's already ingested. They don't want to draw attention—they just want everyone to accept the diagnosis that it was some kind of stroke or preexisting condition. Then Jason can receive whatever therapy he needs for as long as he needs it, and they are no longer culpable."

"Alright. What are you telling me?"

"That they desperately want to know why Jason reacted this way, and they want to know what they can do to prevent this happening again—and how to avoid the inevitable lawsuits that would result. So, of course, they want to keep Jason for testing. I believe you should play along with them until we compile sufficient evidence. That will help allay any suspicions they have that we are preparing a case."

Whitman stared bleakly out the window at the passing streetlights. "We'll do our best."

Confrontation

All the way back across the country, Belknap brooded. He nursed one Martini after another in the comfortable first-class cabin of the 767. In spite of the fact that he had joined forces with other corporations far larger and more powerful than his own, all his lobbying and schmoozing of senators and congressmen for weak or nonexistent GMO laws and permissive labeling requirements was proving to be useless. Even his alliance with the world's largest GMO interest had not worked out well for him. As Niccolo Machiavelli had observed centuries ago, if you ally yourself with someone more powerful, you essentially become their servant. *It's one thing to have laws to keep those big chemical conglomerates under control,* Belknap thought, *but we're doing the Lord's work. We ought to obey God rather than men. We're just doing what we have to do to help people obey God's health laws and to live longer, healthier lives.*

The more he thought about it, the more attractive a facility in South America sounded to him. The laws in Argentina were far more flexible. And this thing with Jason Whitman was just a little too close for comfort. All Belknap needed was some kind of big investigation into what kind of supplements those kids were being given at camp. It was laughable. His research people had been market testing new products on these lucky kids for years, with no bad results. Anyway, for all he knew, Jason's problem was totally unrelated to *Eternal Recall*—the memory-enhancing fern stuff that he hoped would be the next big cash cow. Probably it was some kind of stroke. Or maybe the kid had gotten into some bad weed. He would find out more when he landed and made his way to the clinic.

Jason stared out the window of his clinic room. It was odd—he felt fine physically—full of energy and strength. He didn't remember, of course, that he'd spent the last few weeks in vigorous outdoor activities accompanied by an unequivocally healthful diet. All he knew was that right now he had a major case of cabin fever. He wanted more than anything to get out of this place and get busy. But get busy at what? He couldn't remember. He felt terrific but he had no long-term memory. He knew his immediate family—Mom, Dad, Brandi—to be sure, but his memories of family history were fuzzy. Friends and other relatives—grandparents, aunts, uncles and cousins—were sketchy. Scores of faces and names floated around in his head with no information to attach to them.

Then there were the endless tests. Nurses took vital signs, drew blood and took urine samples every day—sometimes twice a day. Doctors and specialists came in and examined him. Other specialists interviewed him to determine the extent and nature of his memory loss. They would ask him the same questions day after day to see if anything had changed.

Jason's boredom was palpable. He had plenty of video games, and some of those were related to memory tests. The clinic didn't want him watching TV or accessing the Internet because that would color the measurement of his memory. Twice a day they took him downstairs to a gym equipped with the best exercise equipment. Nurses and technicians measured his strength and endurance, which had not flagged. An hour or two on the machines was good, but Jason wanted to be outside, running down the street or a trail or whatever it was he had done in his former life. He really couldn't remember.

As far as Jason was concerned, the one bright spot in the clinic was the food. It was good, solid food. It seemed to be organic and exceptionally tasty.

Once or twice a day his family came to visit him. They could stay as long as they wanted for the most part, but the doctors preferred to conduct some of their tests without the family there. "Please understand," Dr. Waycroft had explained, "we want you to be fully aware of everything we are doing for Jason. It's just that in some instances it's far better for our specialists and technicians to examine him in an environment free of influences that might skew the data. When we arrive at a full diagnosis, and course of treatment, you will be the very first to know."

But of course, Dr. Waycroft already knew what the problem was. And there was no treatment.

———————⟫●⟪———————

It was a chance encounter—so chancy that afterward Marcia was pretty sure it was providential. Brandi was having a play date with a friend and Marcia had stopped at the clinic to visit Jason. He had been there for a day or two and there was no change or progress in his diagnosis. Marcia had stopped at a small, locally owned coffeehouse down the street from the clinic for a latte. This place had been one of Marcia's favorite hangouts for months. Even though it was here in conservatively suburban Vancouver, it had that hippy-esque Portland style of distressed concrete floors, heavily used living room furniture and odd neo-psychedelic tapestries. Across a beat-up coffee table from her she noticed a college-aged girl sprawled in an overstuffed chair with a 24-ounce latte, an I-Pad and dull green textbook generically titled *Clinical Pathology*. On the table in front of her was an open backpack filled with more medical textbooks. An OHSU logo on the backpack suggested she was a medical student at Oregon Health and Science University in Portland.

What made Marcia take notice, however, was her pale green uniform—identical to those at the Wellness 120 clinic. Marcia had never seen this girl there, so she assumed that she worked in a lab or in some other unseen function. If Marcia had not seen her, there was a good chance that she had not seen and would not recognize Marcia. She tried to think of a nonchalant way to start a conversation.

"So it looks like you're slogging through medical school," Marcia began. The girl lowered her book, assessed Marcia, and smiled.

"Yeah," she answered. "Three more years to go. Doing a couple of summer classes to stay ahead of the game. And this is heavy stuff—pathology, diagnosis. So many variables. It's a challenge even for the big-time specialists."

"You're very industrious," Marcia answered.

"Or crazy," snorted the girl. "This summer, on top of the classes, I'm putting in 40 hours a week at a private clinic. Can't tell you where—they like to keep everything totally confidential. I'm a lab assistant, so at least I get to work with some of what I'm learning in school. I just don't have much time left for anything else right now."

"You have my admiration," complimented Marcia. "I don't think I could have done that, even when I was younger. Certainly not now."

"What do you do?" asked the girl, feeling more comfortable with Marcia.

"Oh, I'm a homemaker and a parent. I also do a lot of volunteer work at my kids' schools. Sometimes I feel like I'd like to get back in the paid work force but I'd probably need to get more education. Right out of college I landed a great job in a mortgage company. I just loved it. Had to quit because of chronic fatigue— then as soon as I got over that I had my first kid. That was 17 years ago." Her voice trailed off and she gazed out the window.

"Hmm." The girl gazed out the window herself. "Seventeen years. You know, at my clinic we have a case right now involving a 17-year-old guy. Kind of sad but a little weird."

Marcia tried hard to cover her emotions. She might learn something from this girl that the senior medical staff wasn't telling her. "Really? Why is that?"

"Well," whispered the girl, leaning over the table and laying her textbook aside. "I can't give you any specifics but this kid just totally loses his long-term memory. Out of a clear blue sky. A strong, healthy high school kid. Scary."

"That does sound scary. What do they think it is?"

"That's the thing. They keep telling the family it's a stroke or something like that, but I don't see it. He doesn't have any other signs of any kind of cardiovascular disorder. So I'm thinking what's up with that? Can't they see that? It's kind of like they know the real diagnosis but they just keep saying it's probably a stroke, and then they keep having us do all these tests and evaluations on him."

"What do you think it is?"

"Well, I'm only a second-year med student, but if I had to guess, I'd say he ingested some kind of substance. I dunno. I've only actually seen him twice, and then none of the family was there. He doesn't seem like the kind to do drugs, but maybe he did accidentally or something. Who knows? Anyway I'm not supposed to breathe a word of this to anyone—but you don't even know where I work—and I certainly haven't given you any real specifics."

"No, of course not. But it's an interesting story. And I feel for the family. His parents must be very concerned."

"Yeah, of course."

Marcia looked at her watch and feigned surprise. She wished the girl well in her studies and career. She headed back to her neighborhood a few miles away to pick up Brandi from her play date. She would ask Brandi's friend's mom if Brandi could stay there for dinner. Marcia and Dave had some serious things to discuss with Dr. Waycroft.

On his return to Portland that evening, Belknap wasted no time getting to the clinic. Ida informed him that the Whitmans were talking about moving their son from the clinic to another hospital. At this point, Belknap had no idea that any samples were being tested. His security people had informed him that Bartlett and Whitman had been wandering up a certain trail, and he wondered about that—yet he was pretty sure Bartlett was loyal. Whitman, of course, was looking for answers and that was understandable. Belknap merely needed to steer him and his wife in the right direction.

Meanwhile, Dr. Waycroft had done his best to keep

Jason in the clinic. "Of course you're entitled to a second opinion, or as many as you can afford," he had told the Dave and Marcia. "But look—you're not paying anything here—no deductible—no out of pocket. Dr. Belknap has graciously offered to cover everything and hire the best specialists available. And beyond that—we're right in the middle of some very important, key tests that could mean the difference between your son recovering quickly or not recovering at all. So please, for Jason's sake, keep him here where he can get the best treatment."

Dave and Marcia were in the lobby, quietly talking, when Belknap strode through the front door, accompanied by Ida Morton and Carlton Vance. Marcia suddenly looked up, a bit surprised. Dave wasn't that shocked. If this was the conspiracy he suspected, one might anticipate that it would be a priority for Belknap.

"Dave—Marcia! I'm so very sorry about your son! I heard about him while I was in DC and I was shocked—such a fine young man—I rushed here directly from the airport. But what's this I hear about Jason going to another hospital?"

Belknap's persuasiveness tugged at Dave. He could tell it was going to be an uphill battle to get Jason out of here. "Well, Dr. Belknap, we really appreciate you coming here. Jason is still the same—no memory. We just want to see if another set of doctors would have a different perspective, that's all."

Dr. Waycroft had joined the group and whispered something to Belknap. Belknap nodded. "Dave—you know sometimes these things require patience. 'Let patience have her perfect work,' the Bible says. We pray that God will guide these fine specialists to discover what Jason's affliction is—but we have to have patience.

This could be anything. I know you and Marcia are very diligent about what you eat—but we can never be sure about these rambunctious teenagers, can we?"

Belknap grinned and patted Whitman's arm reassuringly. Whitman did not return the grin. Belknap noticed and flipped his face back to sober. He motioned for the group to be seated in the trendy leather chairs and couch that adorned the lobby.

"Seriously, Dave, we just have to realize that Jason could secretly have been consuming soda pop, sugary coffee drinks, refined snack foods and the like. As I've been saying for decades, those things can have disastrous consequences, and sadly, Jason may be a victim. These are exactly the kinds of things that our specialists here at the clinic can detect—and I can almost guarantee you that they won't look for those things in the big hospitals of the world."

Dave and Marcia were not happy with the course this conversation was taking. It was becoming increasingly hard for them to cover their feelings. By playing the sugar and refined foods card, Belknap seemed to be revealing his desperation. But he didn't seem to be making much headway. He decided to push a bit harder.

"And then there's the other possibility that pains me even to talk about," Belknap said, lowering his voice and drawing closer to the Whitmans. "We all know that even the finest, most moral teenager may be tempted by his friends to experiment with controlled substances. Now—I can't imagine Jason falling to that temptation— and yet we have to realize that he is a youth—and if we eliminate all the other possibilities, the remaining one, no matter how improbable, must be the truth."

By now the Whitmans were livid, yet Belknap's argument was plausible. If they objected, they would seem to be nothing more than doting parents in denial.

Belknap drew even closer and lowered his voice almost to a whisper. "If our specialists here at the clinic were to discover unfortunate traces of such controlled substances in your son's system, we would keep that strictly confidential—on the QT. Yessir, I can warrant you that. We would protect your son's reputation. You know, it's just as important to me as it is to you. But if you take Jason to an outside hospital, you have no such covenant. They find out he's been doing drugs and it'll be right there all over the TV news that same evening. I guarantee it."

Dave thought this was something akin to reverse blackmail. Controlled substances indeed—and Belknap was the pusher! But without bringing up the discoveries (and in the process alerting Belknap to the emerging investigation), Dave couldn't really mount an argument against him. Still, Dave noticed a couple of small beads of perspiration emerging on Belknap's forehead. It was clearer than ever to him that Belknap had something to hide.

Dave looked at Marcia. She reluctantly nodded. "Okay," Dave said, "we'll keep him here for a few more days."

"Wonderful, wonderful!" Belknap smiled, with a little too much relief. "This is really the best thing for Jason, and the best thing for you folks, trust me. Now let's go visit your son."

Jason was busy playing diagnostic computer games, when a knock came at the door. Six people entered. He knew his mom and dad, and of course Dr. Waycroft, whom he didn't exactly trust for some reason. Three others entered: a businesslike woman holding an iPad, a harried looking middle-aged man, and a tall, confident, grinning man in an expensive-looking suit who seemed to be in charge.

"Hello, Jason," began the confident man, extending his hand. Jason studied him for a few seconds and then took his hand and shook it solidly. "Do you remember me, Jason?"

"No. But you look important. Are you the head dude around here?"

The group laughed quietly. "Well, yes, I guess you might say I'm the head dude," chuckled the man. "I'm Dr. Tyler Belknap, and I'm president of Wellness 120. I've been your dad's boss since before you were born."

If Belknap expected a warm and positive reaction from Jason, he was disappointed. Jason's eyes grew wide, and his face contracted into a scowl. He stepped back, knocking over the rolling stand and laptop on which he had been working, raised his hand and pointed at Belknap. "It's you!"

"Yes, it's me," Belknap answered, perplexed.

"You're the one the guy in the forest told me about! My Dad's boss! You've been using people to experiment with all kinds of weird chemicals in food. You're the one who made me lose my memory! And you've been telling people lies! But it's all gonna be over soon! You're gonna be out of the picture and some other people are gonna come in and take over and change things! There'll be new laws to protect people from scammers like you!"

The jaws of everyone in the room dropped. Dave and Marcia both shot glances at the other four whose reactions were a rapid sequence of surprise, guilt, terror and anger. Belknap regained his composure and reached a hand out to Jason, "Son, you're confused. Those were simply hallucinations. Just calm down."

Jason had already picked up the little table on which the laptop had been. He swung the table at Belknap. Belknap jumped back. Waycroft had already motioned for two security guards to come in. They grabbed Jason, pushed him down and pinned him firmly to the bed. Orderlies arrived with straps to subdue him. Another nurse entered with a hypodermic needle, followed by an assistant—the girl that Marcia had talked to in the coffee shop. The girl spotted Marcia and gaped, momentarily.

"Hey! Let my son go!" shouted Whitman, moving forward. One of the security guards blocked him.

"Just as a precaution to keep him from hurting himself," said Waycroft. "This is a simple sedative. It will calm him and make him go to sleep." Waycroft took the needle from the nurse, snapped it with his finger a couple of times and squirted it in the air. Then, as the orderlies held Jason's arm steady, Waycroft found a vein, rubbed it and slipped the needle in. Jason's struggles subdued and his eyelids began to close. He mumbled something that sounded like "Jesus" and passed out. But it wasn't an expletive.

———⟫●⟪———

Bartlett sat at his breakfast table with his morning coffee and newspaper, but his mind wasn't on the headlines.

The Whitmans had called Bartlett the night before and told him about Marcia's chance encounter with the lab assistant. They also filled him in on Belknap's visit to the clinic, Jason's shocking statements and the near violence that ensued. Was Jason's meeting with the man in the forest a hallucination? Bartlett didn't think so. It would be hard for any coffee-guzzling pro fiction writer to come up with stuff like this, let alone a severely memory-impaired adolescent, especially when the "hallucination" comported so well with the truth that was now emerging.

Bartlett's rumination was interrupted with a call

from Dr. Tracy Horton at WSU. She and her staff had completed tests on the material that Bartlett and Whitman had brought her. Yes, there were several compounds that could be associated with GMOs. Of course this didn't mean conclusively that they had come from a GMO—just that they might have. And even if they did, there was nothing illegal at this point about selling foods or supplements that had been derived from GMOs (although falsely claiming that GMO products were non-GMO would be another matter). In every case, the compounds were in a form that was not isolated or synthetic—they were part of a plant. Of special interest were capsules with, among other things, leaves and spores from *gymnocarpium dryopteris*—the northern oak fern, reputed in some folk medicine traditions to have very mild psychoactive properties. These particular leaves and spores contained excessive amounts of an unusual alkaloid, possibly psychoactive.

On a hunch, Dr. Horton had walked out the door of her lab, picked a few sprigs of northern oak fern growing along the fence, and compared the results. The quantity of the alkaloid in that sample was only a tiny fraction of what it was in the capsule Bartlett and Whitman had obtained from the file cabinets in the Conference Center kitchen. Again, this didn't point conclusively to a GMO, but there had to be a reason for the vastly differing proportions of the alkaloid.

Bartlett sat and considered. Suddenly it was all coming together. He hadn't really wanted this to happen but he knew that many cults or cultic groups typically conform to a model of exponential growth followed by a period of relative corporate stability, followed by some crisis (a failed prediction or scandal) in which the group either collapses or takes on a different form—

or, in rare cases, is re-formed. He prayed for wisdom—on his part and on the part of local, state and federal authorities. He prayed for the Whitmans, for Jason—and even for Belknap and his cronies. There was still time for them to do the right thing and to come clean.

But still, there was a time for justice to be served, so that more people wouldn't get hurt. Bartlett pulled his laptop toward him and Googled the United States Food and Drug Administration—Portland Office. Then he picked up his phone and started dialing.

<hr/>

The air that morning in Belknap's office was thick with foreboding. Belknap sat at his huge desk, bitter black coffee in hand. Vance and Patrick sat in a couple of the semicircle of chairs facing him. The huge semicircle of windows behind Belknap revealed a dark grey sky pouring down rain.

"I'm thinking it wouldn't be a good idea to *fire* Whitman, but we could have Richardson pay him a visit to help him get his family in line," Patrick concluded.

Belknap shot a look of utter contempt at Patrick. "You idiot! This has gone beyond our usual tactics. It's just getting out of control."

"What about that stuff the kid said last night? If it's not his family, someone else must have put him up to it. Richardson can take care of them, for sure."

Belknap's eyes rolled to the ceiling. "What are you—Al Capone's grandkid? Didn't you hear me? We can't fix this one by pushing people around. It's getting worse and its getting out of our control. And beyond that—the federal and state governments aren't cooperating with us like they used to. It's time to cut our losses."

"I don't know," said Vance. "I think if we act quickly, we still have plenty of time to get rid of any—uh—

evidence, before any cops come knocking on our door. It's worth a shot. And then if that doesn't work...."

Connie Kerwyn, an FDA investigator working out of the Beaverton, Oregon office was, to say the least, shocked to get a call from an actual board member of Wellness 120. For years she had wondered why Wellness 120 products seemed to have been off limits for her office. And now, suddenly, an executive in the organization seemed to be blowing the whistle. Apparently he had potentially incriminating evidence which had already been analyzed by the WSU Vancouver lab. It seemed that supplements given to at least one summer camp attendee at Wellness 120's Retreat Center in the Cascade foothills contained psychoactive compounds. The lab further noted that the compounds were possibly derived from GMOs. Additionally, the alleged victim was being treated for severe long-term memory loss at a private Wellness 120 clinic.

To Kerwyn, this was both horrifying and fascinating. She had plenty of work waiting in her inbox, but this one seemed urgent, and she was free to initiate investigations if she thought the situation warranted it. In this case, there might be several possible violations, although some of them would be challenging to prove, and not all of them would be in her purview. A few calls to alert her friends at other federal, state and local agencies would be in order.

Two days later, Kerwyn and her associates from other agencies, along with Clark County Sheriff's deputies, showed up at the Retreat Center, warrants in hand. They quickly secured the kitchen and rummaged through file cabinets, which of course had already been cleared of the campers' supplements. They confiscated computers and records. They confiscated food samples.

Then, acting on information provided by Bartlett and Whitman, they returned to the parking lot and approached the gate at the other side. To their surprise it was open. Up the trail, they came to a heavy iron gate. It was open as well. After another quarter-mile they arrived in a box canyon with a waterfall cascading down the far end. There, in the nearly vertical wall of the canyon, was the entrance to an old silver mine, blocked with a massive camo-green steel door dotted with heavy rivets. The investigators were examining the cardkey box at the door's side, considering how they were going to gain entry, short of a direct hit by a cruise missile, when the door slowly and quietly opened of its own accord. The party cautiously stepped inside, to discover a clean, brightly lit office environment, with a hall stretching back into the hillside. A figure emerged from a door down the hall, and walked toward them. It was none other than the grinning Tyler Belknap himself.

"Hello, folks! Welcome to our confidential research facility here at Wellness 120. After your hike up the trail you must be thirsty. Help yourself to fresh spring water, or a variety of organic juices if you prefer."

Belknap began to shake hands with members of the group, who looked a little confused. Kerwyn handed Belknap a search warrant. Belknap took it, skimmed it over and handed it to his general counsel, Robert Hargrove, who took his time reading each line while investigators and deputies waited. Hargrove whispered something to Belknap.

"Thanks, Bob," said Belknap. "Well, everything seems to be in order here, Ms..."

"Kerwyn. Investigator Kerwyn with the FDA. We ..."

"I understand, Ms. Kerwyn. Our research facility is completely open to you. Please take samples of anything you like. If you have any questions, feel free to talk to any of our staff. They'll make sure everything you take is labeled correctly. And of course I'm here along with our CLO, Robert Hargrove, our Director of Research and Development, Dr. Steve Capell and our capable Information Officer Dawson Criswell, to answer any general questions you may have."

There were brief huddles between the various agents. A couple of them took Belknap up on his offer of water and juice, while others looked on disapprovingly. Then they spread out and went about their business of exploring the facility and collecting samples. Again, they examined the computers, removing the hard drives from some machines, and confiscating documents from file cabinets.

Through all this, Belknap and his staff remained strangely unperturbed, calm and cooperative. Kerwyn couldn't help but notice this. "Dr. Belknap, we appreciate your cooperation but I hope this is not some sort of ploy to throw us off the trail somehow, because we will discover whether or not you've been mislabeling GMOs, and whether or not you've been testing your GMOs or other isolated substances on the children at your summer camp."

Belknap smiled and nodded. "I understand your concern. And that's precisely why we are cooperating. We have nothing to lose and everything to gain, since your investigation will demonstrate clearly to the public that Wellness 120 is one hundred percent law-abiding! In fact, we answer to a Higher Source. Our ethics are beyond human law."

Kerwyn regarded Belknap for a moment or two, and then turned and went about her business. In all of her years of dealing with slick, manipulative people, this man was the slickest. His religious exterior was polished to perfection. She could sense this was merely a facade, yet if anything was to be done about it, she needed enough evidence to make a clear and convincing case. And now she had the distinct feeling that any such evidence had either been spirited away or rendered irrelevant by Belknap's attorneys.

Aftermath

Two weeks after the initial investigations, Kerwyn was still slogging through the data. Some of the supplements that Bartlett and Whitman had gathered, and that the WSU lab had analyzed, did in fact contain an unusual alkaloid—probably psychoactive but not on any list of controlled substances. But since the law does not require dietary supplements to be reviewed by the FDA before marketing, there was no violation—unless a new ingredient was included. It was clear that Belknap was attempting to circumvent the requirement by engineering the plant in which the additive was found.

With supplements (unlike drugs), the *manufacturer* is responsible for ensuring the safety of a product. If there are complaints, the FDA is responsible for demonstrating that the product is *unsafe*. But the law also requires the manufacturers to report consumer complaints of adverse effects to the FDA. Kerwyn suspected that Belknap and his gang had been sweeping complaints under the carpet for a long time and for a lot of products. If she could prove that, she would have plenty of reason for legal action.

As for testing psychoactive substances on campers without their permission and the permission of their families, FDA standards for informed consent documents are clear. Belknap's legal team had attempted to weave informed consent for product testing into the documents for the Summer Institute. FDA lawyers were studying the documents and preparing a case.

Likewise, Belknap's legal team had done a valiant job at skirting FDA and USDA labeling requirements for foods and supplements. They were making non-organic ingredients seem to be organic, and GMOs seem to be non-GMO, without actual USDA certification.

Otherwise, the investigation had moved into interviews and depositions with key personnel and with campers at the Summer Institute. Belknap and his loyal troops had done a superb job of cleaning everything up and removing any potentially damaging evidence.

Anything of value (or potentially incriminating) to the investigation was almost certainly safely deposited in an undisclosed location. Kerwyn had demanded formulas for every Wellness 120 product. Early on, Vance had provided her with an extensive list, but Kerwyn suspected it had been edited. Without more complete information, it would take investigators a while to assemble a narrative as to what was really happening at Wellness 120.

Meanwhile, Dave and Marcia had taken Jason to a conventional hospital for examination, along with information on what substances he may have ingested. Doctors called in specialists and conducted more tests, but the results were inconclusive. After a few days, Jason went home. Other than the identity of his family, he still couldn't remember anything prior to waking up in the forest in the middle of the night. Any memories earlier than that were simply gone—or uselessly out of context. Disconnected facts, figures and images floated and tossed around in his head like so many rudderless, anchorless dinghies in a storm. He retained many of his skills from before, but he had no idea where or when he had acquired them. He knew he was an American, but didn't know where America was or, for that matter, any other country in the world. His sister Brandi had tried hard to fill her brother in—but nothing much seemed to stick.

As far as details of the events after Jason's long-term memory loss, he remembered nearly everything, including the details of his wandering in the forest and his rescue. He still insisted that he had talked to some guy named Josh out in the woods who had encouraged him, fed him the best grilled trout ever, and warned him about Belknap.

Dave and Marcia were discouraged. Yes, blood tests at the hospital had shown traces of the same psychoactive compound that Dr. Horton at WSU had found in one of the capsules recovered from Jason's stash. Yet the compound was unique enough that few if any studies had been done on it. Jason's symptoms could not be conclusively blamed on the compound. Without a clear diagnosis, the doctors couldn't predict much about Jason's recovery. One hopeful prospect was that federal and state investigators had subpoenaed Jason's records from the Wellness 120 clinic, and had interviewed Dr. Waycroft extensively. Perhaps that line of inquiry would provide more information—but that still didn't mean a cure.

The more time passed, the more discouraged and angry Dave and Marcia became. They had been taken for a giant ride for two decades—thinking they were involved in something worthwhile, thinking they were serving their fellow human beings and serving God. The idea of living 120 years and extreme longevity in general—ideas on which Belknap had built his company—now seemed pointless and absurd. To Dave it seemed like yet another myth imposed by big business (including the big business of religion) and promoted by advertising and the media, of which Dave was a part. And now the whole thing was falling apart around them. Even that might have been tolerable, had it not fallen directly on their son's head.

The worst part of all this was that Belknap and his cronies didn't seem to care. Whitman had seen hardly any of them since their awkward visit to the clinic, and Jason's near-violent accusation. Belknap continued to tape his *120 Club* program as if nothing were wrong. He cloistered himself in his office along with Vance, Patrick and Ida Morton. They left the day-to-day operations to the managers. The board of directors had even conducted a meeting without Vance, Patrick and Belknap present. Whitman had the distinct feeling this was a lull before some kind of organizational cataclysm.

⸺⸺⸺

"I wish I had better news, but there's just not enough of the right kind of evidence for a case—at least not yet." Kerwyn thought she should call Bartlett and let him know what was going on, something she normally would not have done. In this case, she thought he deserved to be in the loop, as a board member who had provided evidence of wrongdoing within the organization. "We're moving in the right direction, but we're getting a lot of stonewalling. No one will directly admit anything."

"So what do we do now?" asked Bartlett.

"Keep doing what you're doing and we'll keep pressing everyone we think might know something. Eventually, the truth is bound to come out."

Bartlett felt like things were grinding to a halt, or

hanging in midair. Choose your metaphor. In any case, the organization couldn't go back to the way it was.

He suddenly felt a need to be proactive about the organization's image. He decided it was time to pay a friendly visit to Dawson Criswell.

Criswell was fighting an increasingly uphill battle to put a positive spin on day-to-day developments within the organization. He took his orders directly from the top, but the organization had been mostly topless in the last few weeks. Criswell didn't always know where the bodies were buried or if there *were* any bodies. He didn't really care. His job was to get his key message into the media. He relentlessly transformed anything else— any question, any allegation—into his key message—that Wellness 120 was an upstanding organization dedicated to serving God and humanity, extending human lifespans to that which God had ordained.

Bartlett quietly appeared at Criswell's open door. Criswell, busily engaged in creating a press release, didn't even notice him standing there. After studying Criswell for a while, Bartlett cleared his throat. Startled, Criswell looked up, rapidly masking his stressed face with an almost Belknapish grin. "Clifford, my friend, good morning! My apologies—I was preoccupied! How may I be of service today?"

"Oh, no no no, Dawson—how may *I* be of service to *you*? May I come in?"

"Sure—have a seat. Are we having fun yet?"

"I conjecture that neither of us are currently having as much fun as we've had in the past, yet I have every confidence that we will be having more fun in the future." Bartlett smiled wryly.

"I'm encouraged, then," replied Criswell.

"I just bet you've been hammered with questions on certain topics of late."

"Uh huh. Want to guess which?"

"I'll take a stab," said Bartlett. "One—the status of the Whitman boy. Two—the ongoing investigation into our ingredients and labeling. Three—did Wellness 120 actually test psychoactive substances on youths without the consent of them or their families? Four—why are Mr. Belknap, Mr. Patrick, Mr. Vance and Ms. Morton becoming increasingly scarce lately?"

"Remarkable. Okay—here goes. One—Jason Whitman is not in the care of our organization at this point, so I can't speak to that question with any degree of authority. Wellness 120 is of course concerned for his health and well-being, and we pray for his speedy recovery. Two—at Wellness 120 we take the utmost care with the quality of our products and the information we provide for the people we serve. Three—the Wellness 120 Summer Institute has traditionally been a venue where we have offered our forthcoming products to young participants, because we value their input. We would never knowingly allow them to ingest psychoactive substances. Four—as to the busy schedules of our officers and board members, I know they are, as always, prayerfully working themselves to the point of exhaustion to make sure that Wellness 120 continues to produce the very finest health and longevity products available anywhere. I am, of course, not privy to the content or outcome of all their meetings, but, knowing them as I do, I personally trust that wise and sagacious decisions are emerging every minute they are on the job—decisions that will be of lasting benefit to each and every one of our valued customers. We are well aware of the ongoing investigations, and we are fully cooperating with every constituted authority, just as God's word instructs us to. We want to insure that there are no miscreants within our ranks."

Bartlett grinned sardonically. "My goodness, Dawson! You are right on top of your game. I am nearly moved to tears at your prosaic grandeur. But I wonder if it's not time for us to alter our official position on these topics a bit."

"How so, Clifford? I'm merely holding to the position that Dr. Belknap personally approved."

"And how long ago was that?"

"Oh—about two weeks, I think."

"Mm-hmm. So—right after the initial investigations—and Belknap's obfuscatory stonewalling at our clandestine research facility."

"Please, Clifford. That facility is—was until recently anyway—confidential for understandable security and safety reasons. I didn't even know it existed. And apparently you didn't either until you wandered up the wrong trail with Whitman. There was nothing wrong going on there."

"Dawson—you don't need to be defensive toward me and you don't need to speak the party line. You and I both know that things are changing—that the outcome of the investigations will probably show that there has been some major wrongdoing. If you haven't been subpoenaed yet you will be, and you'd better tell them everything you know."

"All I know is what I hear from Dr. Belknap."

"Well, and that's exactly the problem isn't it? Dawson, just a question for you—don't you think we need to change the tone of our public information and press releases to drop the fortress mentality and allow for the eventuality of something big happening in the near future?"

Criswell rose to his feet. "Dr. Bartlett, you disappoint me. It sounds like someone got up on the wrong side of the bed this morning! You should try our *Psalm*

118:24 Organic Carob Brownies. This is the day which the Lord hath made; we will rejoice and be glad in it. With our special herbal blend, you'll start every day happy! And while there is an ongoing investigation, you will recall that the various agencies have found nothing. Nothing at all. The minute we are presented with something, we will act. Until that happens (and we have no reason to believe it will) we will continue with our mission of producing the best health and longevity products available anywhere."

Bartlett thanked Criswell for his time, and headed back to his office. To his surprise, Criswell believed his own press releases more than the public did. Yet Bartlett hoped he had planted a seed.

———⋙●⋘———

A week later, three weeks after Jason's "accident," Belknap, Patrick, Vance and Morton didn't show up for work. Instead, an envelope was delivered by messenger service at precisely 8:00 am to Wellness 120 headquarters, addressed to the board of directors. At 10:00 am a special meeting of the board was convened.

Inside the envelope were four letters, signed and notarized. The first one was from Tyler Belknap, resigning from his presidency, the board and the organization. The second two, from Vance and Patrick, followed suit. The fourth, from Ida Morton, simply offered a resignation from the company.

On examining the letters, three board members tendered their resignations on the spot. In the absence of a president and CEO, the remaining board immediately elected Clifford Bartlett to fill those positions. Bartlett's first action was to notify the authorities of the change in administration.

But Belknap and his buddies were nowhere to be found. Investigators, suspecting some foul play, had obtained a warrant to enter Belknap's posh home over-looking the Columbia River. The elegant home looked as if it was still lived in—food in the refrigerator—clothing in the closet. A maid and a gardener, arriving in the morning, were surprised to find investigators hard at work. The maid confirmed that some of Belknap's clothing and several of his suitcases seemed to be missing. Personal records, documents, computers and storage media were gone. An attorney arrived and informed investigators that the home had been placed on the market, and that the proceeds were to be donated to a Portland charity.

Similar arrangements had been made for Vance, Patrick and Morton, although Vance and Patrick gifted their personal estates to their nieces and nephews.

Since they were persons of interest in an ongoing investigation, police immediately checked passenger lists at PDX. Nothing. Flights from all U.S. and Canadian airports. Nothing. Recent credit card usage. Nothing. No one had any information. Belknap and his crew had vanished into the atmosphere. They were simply gone—although it would be several days before they could be officially classified as missing persons.

Bartlett was not entirely surprised with this turn of events. He suspected that rather than face criminal charges, Belknap and his group would cut their losses and run, although he had no idea where. Belknap had split none too soon. Just two days after his disappearance and resignation letter, Bartlett got a call from Kerwyn.

"All the information is in, and it has all been analyzed," said Kerwyn. We're going to cite your company on 156 counts of fraudulent labeling. Further, we found psychoactive or potentially addictive ingredients in at least 35 products—that present a clear safety risk."

"That many?"

"Afraid so."

Bartlett was disheartened. He knew there were problems, of course, but he had no idea of the scope of what had been going on, apparently for years. His work was cut out for him. It meant a review of every product. Hundreds of thousands of products in Wellness 120 warehouses, outlets and other retailers across the country would need to be recalled or relabeled. The task was mind-boggling. It also meant a major publicity campaign to let the public know that Wellness 120 was reforming and transforming.

In the meantime, sales would plummet. Bartlett and his management team would need to stay ahead of the game by closing outlets, liquidating assets, and unfortunately laying off employees. Maybe, just maybe, it would be possible to avoid bankruptcy. Maybe, just maybe, it would be possible to rebuild, reinvent and reposition the corporation as a genuine, honest maker of wholesome food products—without the misapplied spiritual coercion and false promises that Belknap had used for so many years.

Bartlett realized that all the dishonesty, experimentation, manipulation—the legal and criminal issues—were not the main problems. They were merely festering symptoms of a much deeper problem—*bad religion*.

Kerwyn, still on the line, interrupted Bartlett's thoughts. "Dr. Bartlett—are you there?"

"Oh…yes…sorry. What have you found out about testing on the campers?"

"Well, as much as your corporate attorneys tried to weasel out of it, they failed to acquire proper informed consent. We're citing the company for at least 300 counts of failure to obtain informed consent before using a human subject in a clinical trial. That's just for the last three years. It will probably be more as we gather evidence for earlier Summer Institutes. We don't know how far back this practice goes. You'll be subpoenaed for a deposition, by the way, if you already haven't been."

It was disturbing news, but again, Bartlett was not at all surprised. It confirmed what he and many others had suspected for years. Bartlett sighed, "At least we're getting things resolved. What about Jason Whitman?"

"That's a whole other can of worms, involving violations of federal, state and local laws. But as I understand it, our medical consultants have sifted through all the tests that were done on Jason Whitman in the Wellness 120 clinic, and compared them to his tests at other medical facilities. It looks like the Wellness 120 clinic was just buying time, and trying to come up with some evidence that would show he had had a stroke or had taken drugs or something like that. They're indicting Waycroft and a couple of other employees at the clinic. Our people are almost certain that Jason's brain injuries are due to the substances he ingested at the summer camp. We'll have expert testimony on that."

"Now you're calling it a brain injury?" asked Bartlett.

"Yes—that's what it is."

⟫⟩●⟨⟪

Dave and Marcia Whitman sat in their living room with their son and daughter. It was a September Sunday morning—one of those clear, fresh days that makes Pacific Northwesterners put up with the nine months of overcast and rain. Dave and Marcia were sipping coffee. Jason was skimming through a large, illustrated book on US history, thumbing through a section on the Founding Fathers. He had no idea who these people were. Brandi was sitting next to him, offering basic facts about Thomas Jefferson, Benjamin Franklin and George Washington, James Monroe and others. "Why do they all have long hair?" Jason asked. "Were they musicians?"

Dave, Marcia and Brandi laughed. Jason looked puzzled. It was a bittersweet moment—one of many every day. Jason lacked much of the fundamental, background knowledge we take for granted. He was slowly relearning it, but there was so much to relearn. The days when he seemed to be making progress were sometimes offset by days when he made none—a step forward and a step back.

"Dad, why do we live in this house—and in this town?"

"We moved to this house about 15 years ago. And we live in the Portland area because your grandparents moved here in the 50s. Your mom and I grew up here and met in the 80s. We got married in 1990 and I started working for Wellness 120 a couple of years later. I've worked there ever since."

"Why did you go to work for an evil man like Belknap? Weren't there other places you could have landed a job?"

Jason hadn't said a word about Belknap since his confrontation with him that night in the clinic. Ironically, Dave and Marcia *hoped*, if Jason were going to have memory problems, that incident would be a good one to forget.

"Well, I did have a job in an ad agency—and a pretty good one at that. But at the time, Belknap seemed like a good man. His products and his books had helped your mom feel a whole lot better. And it just seemed like a good place to work—a place where I could make more of a difference than I could working in an ad agency."

"Well, the guy in the forest told me otherwise—that it wasn't really a good place."

Marcia was staring at the floor, crying. She was still unsure if Jason's encounter in the forest was a real event. She really wanted to believe it—because it would confirm to her that *Someone* was overseeing their situation.

Twenty years ago Belknap had cured Marcia of her chronic fatigue, or so she thought at the time. Now she didn't know what to think. If her illness had grown, there was a chance that she never would have had her two wonderful kids. Maybe this was a matter of the Lord giving and the Lord taking away. Anyway, as long as Jason was alive and in good health, there was a chance that he could kick this thing—that he could re-learn what he had forgotten. Or maybe it was all still in there and just couldn't be accessed and maybe the doctors would discover a way to do that. She didn't know. It was the uncertainty that got to her. She could see that it was getting to Dave as well, but he was trying hard to cover it up and to provide an image of strength and security for his family.

Meanwhile, Jason was looking intently at something out the window. Suddenly, he stood up and ran to the window for a better look. "It's him."

"It's who?" asked Marcia.

There was a knock at the door. Marcia and Dave looked at each other.

"I'll get it," Brandi said, already running for the door.

"No, wait, Brandi. You don't know who's out there. Let your dad answer..." But it was too late. Brandi had already opened the door and was staring up at a man with a canvas jacket, jeans and hiking boots. He had a short, dark beard, longish black hair, and a few scars and pockmarks on his face. He seemed to wear a very friendly expression.

"Brandi! It's good to see you. Is Jason here?" the man asked.

"Yes, of course he is," answered Brandi. "He can't really go anywhere because he doesn't remember things. He would get lost."

Dave had arrived at the door. He regarded the man with apprehension. He wondered if the man might be homeless, but his clothing didn't look *that* worn and he seemed to be neatly groomed. Also, the man exuded an intelligent confidence and friendliness that wasn't part of the stereotypical homeless persona. "How do you know my son's and daughter's names?" asked Dave.

"I'm well acquainted with them. You might say I'm a teacher," answered the man. "May I come in?"

That answer didn't satisfy Dave. If anything, it raised more questions. But the man's demeanor seemed so—*safe*—that Dave conceded. "Sure. Come on in. What did you say your name was?"

"Josh. Call me Josh." Josh extended his hand to Marcia and Dave who both shook it.

Meanwhile, Jason was standing in the middle of the room, staring wide-eyed. "It's you—the man in the forest!"

Dave cast a concerned glance at Marcia, who took a couple of steps back and put her hand to her gaping mouth.

"Jason! I see you made it back to civilization—and I see that the man I told you about is out of the picture for now."

"Just like you said. And I'm not getting much better, just like you said."

"I know, Jason," Josh put a reassuring hand on Jason's shoulder. "But you will. And this will all be worthwhile."

Dave and Marcia were looking back and forth between Jason and Josh. "Are you talking about Belknap? How do you know about that? Hey—are you really the guy he keeps talking about that was in the forest when he was lost?"

"Yes, in fact, I am!" Josh grinned a sincere grin and nodded at Jason. "He needed encouragement at the time. And also a breakfast of trout, right Jason? You were pretty hungry."

Dave was still having a lot of trouble with all of this. Meanwhile Josh's talk of food reminded Marcia of hospitality. "Would you like something to eat? We haven't had breakfast yet. I could fix some scrambled eggs and toast—all organic."

Josh grinned again. "That would be wonderful, Marcia. May I help you? I know what Jason would like, but I don't have any fish with me just now."

"Ewww!" grimaced Brandi. "*Fish for breakfast*? I'd rather have eggs!"

Josh laughed. "Well, you know, if your kid asks for an egg, what are you gonna do? Hey—I have an incredible omelet that I create. Can I do that for you? Would that be okay, Marcia? I'll do the eggs if you do everything else."

"I guess so. I won't object to anyone cooking for me." Josh and Marcia went into the kitchen area and went to work, Brandi started setting the table and Dave and Jason sat and watched.

"So tell me," Dave said to Josh, "what was the deal up there in the woods? Did you just run into Jason—or did you somehow know where he was?"

"I had a job for Jason—I still do—and he needed to know what was going on," answered Josh. "He needed to know that all the trouble he was going through was going to produce something good. And I'm truly sorry that all of this had to happen. Now you *all* need encouragement. But right up front, you need to know that Jason's condition won't improve much in the near future."

"How do you know that and how the heck is it encouraging?" asked Dave, frowning.

Josh was standing at the range, adroitly tossing eggs and other ingredients into a skillet as if he were a master chef at one of the world's finest restaurants. Using the pan, he flipped an omelet without spilling a particle of egg or a drop of oil. Without breaking his stride, Josh answered, "It's encouraging because you know that your suffering contributes to a positive outcome. Jason's brain injury from the ingestion of that substance has led directly to the reform of Wellness 120 and the exposure and resignations of Belknap and his gang. That means a lot of people who were struggling and confused will no longer be—including yourselves."

Dave couldn't counter that argument. "Josh, you talked to Jason up there on the hill when he was lost. How come you didn't just lead him back to his camp? Or call for help on your cell phone?"

"Actually, Jason needed a few more hours in my forest before he got back to the chaotic world of human beings. And I don't have a cell phone. Don't need one."

"So you just left him there?"

"Sure. You should spend more time up there yourselves. There's nothing like my forest—or any kind of wilderness, really—to get you in touch with my Dad, don't you think?"

Marcia paused from stacking toast on a plate. "What do you mean? Your dad lives up there? Your family owns the land? I thought Wellness 120 owned it. And I thought you said you were a teacher."

"You might say I'm the landlord. Look, I know

you're depressed and worried about Jason. I'm just here to tell you that he's going to be fine in the long run, but his life is not going to take the course you had in mind. I could arrange it that way, but the *best* plan is that for several more years he will be a reminder to people of the kind of damage that a false promise can do to sincere people when it's painted the color of religion. He trusts me on this. If you folks trust me, you'll be surprised how much better you'll feel."

Brandi had set the table and Marcia had finished placing a plate of toast, a jar of blueberry preserves and a bowl of orange sections in the center. Josh came from the kitchen with a plate of five perfect omelets, filled with something. He slid one onto each plate. The group sat down at the table. Dave offered a brief prayer of thanks and put a forkful of omelet in his mouth.

"I'm still not sure..." began Dave. "Oh my gosh! This is incredible!"

Marcia was stunned. It looked like a normal vegetable omelet with some kind of cheese sauce, produced with ingredients from her refrigerator and spice rack, but the flavor was almost dizzying. "Where did you learn to cook like this?"

"I'm glad you like it, said Josh. "It's really nothing much. I suppose you could say I have a pretty good working knowledge of chemistry, biology, physics—you know—the way everything works together. Food, nutrition and health really don't have to be a big, complicated thing. Human bodies weren't designed to last forever anyway. Just through this world."

The Whitmans were savoring the omelets and now trying to absorb what Josh was saying. But Dave wanted to finish his earlier thought. "Josh—what you said before—what are we supposed to be trusting you to do? Do you have some connection with Belknap?"

"Oh, I'm connected to just about everyone, but not everyone wants to be connected to me. It might look to you like Belknap and his gang are getting off 'scott free.' But they won't." Josh shook his head and stared out the window. "They're in Argentina right now building a factory and an international supplement business that will be bigger than the operation they had here, and a whole lot more dangerous. You won't find them under the names they used here. They don't even look the same. They've covered their tracks pretty well, and it cost 'em a ton of money to do it. But they have a mint from their earlier shenanigans before they even settled here in Vancouver."

"I don't understand what you do," said Marcia. "First you claimed to be a teacher—then you said you were a landowner—you seem to know something about everything and now you know about Belknap. "How do you know all this stuff? Are you with the FBI or something?"

Josh laughed—a big, healthy laugh. "Really—do you know that's the first time in history I've ever been asked that question? No. I'm not FBI, CIA or NSA. I'm not spying on you and I'm not monitoring your texts, emails or phones."

"I don't see what's so funny," said Dave. "I just want to see Belknap and his gang brought to justice."

"If justice is really what you want, don't worry. They may not be 'brought to justice'—but justice will find them. No question about that. Everyone will have to face what they have done and what they have not done, and how their actions have affected other people. Everyone will understand. And then they will face the grace of God."

"Well—that's not exactly what I meant…"

"I know, Dave. You're concerned that they won't be brought before the human court system. And as I know that you know, the human justice system doesn't deliver real justice or real mercy. That comes only from God. And it *will* come. And the suffering that your son and so many others have endured as a result of these people will be resolved. Jason is going to be okay—he's going to be excellent—he's going to be perfect—in my good time."

"In your *good time*?" Dave wanted to make sure he had heard right.

Dave and Marcia exchanged skeptical glances.

"Yeah—it really is good. Here's the thing. This isn't a good world. It's a world of free will where all kinds of bad things happen. Mistakes, accidents, disasters, wars, crime and so forth. It's not pretty. We all suffer. Jason suffers, you suffer, little kids suffer. I've suffered. What do you think, Marcia? Why doesn't God do something?"

Marcia looked uncomfortable at being put on the spot. "I just don't know. I've always wondered about it, but no one has ever given me a good answer—one that I feel comfortable with. Some people say all the suffering in the world is just because we have free will and because we sin. But it still seems like God is ultimately responsible for the whole thing, because he created the potential for it to happen. I'm sorry—I can't really get past that thought. Especially when I think about Jason." Marcia looked like she was going to cry.

"You know," Josh pointed at the ceiling, "most people think of God as someone way up above the world—separate from it. In one sense he is, but at the same time he is not. He's right here with you. They also think of him as some kind of big honcho, giving orders—rewarding people who make him happy and punishing people who upset him. He's not that way."

"What way is he?" asked Brandi.

"He serves."

Brandi frowned. "What do you mean?"

"He serves his creation. He takes care of it. He takes care of you. He takes care of everyone. He's a servant. It's what he does."

"Okay," said Marcia. "If that's right, there are sure a lot of people who seem to be falling through the cracks. It still doesn't explain why a totally powerful God allows such horrible things to happen to people."

Josh looked Marcia in the eye. "Maybe God wants you to discover what it is to be like Him—to be servants. But how could you learn that in a perfect world where there's no suffering—no problems, no needs, no service? So maybe that's why, instead of fixing everything, he comes here to experience this imperfect human life and to suffer with you, before he takes you into the next life."

"True dat," agreed Jason. "You should know."

Marcia and Dave looked at Jason, perplexed. "We'll have to give that some thought," said Dave. "This is kind of hard to get our heads around."

"You will," affirmed Josh. "Well, folks, it's time for me to go." He got up from the table and began to collect dishes.

Marcia looked horrified. "What are you doing?"

"It would be rude of me to leave you with all these dishes. Besides, on a day like today you don't want to be stuck inside. Get out and do something. And take Mrs. Mohler with you. She lives three houses to the south. She's been feeling a little down lately—needs some cheering up." Josh was already rinsing dishes at the sink and loading them in the dishwasher. "This'll only take a minute or two. Here, Brandi. You can help me dry these pans."

Brandi grabbed a towel from the rack and began to dry. As Josh cleaned up the kitchen, she chatted about school and friends. Josh inserted comments, seeming to know exactly who and what she was talking about. Jason was still sitting at the table smiling and seeming to know what was happening. Dave and Marcia were sitting across from him looking bewildered. Finally Josh laid the towel aside and moved toward the front door. The family followed.

"Remember—just a little while and then everything and everyone will be restored. I guarantee it. I'll be looking in on you frequently—all the time, actually. No wiretapping, cell phone monitoring or drones though," Josh chuckled. He shook Dave and Marcia's hands, hugged Jason and Brandi, walked to the front door and opened it.

"Where's your car?" asked Dave, peering out the door.

"Oh, I don't need a car. Walking works just fine for me. A pretty amazing idea, even if I do say so myself." He proceeded out of the front yard and down the sidewalk.

"Hey, Josh," called Dave. "You didn't give us any contact info. When can we get in touch with you? Are you local?"

Josh didn't answer but laughed his big, healthy laugh, and waved as he disappeared around the corner. The family stood on the front porch. Brandi was grinning and seemed a lot less stressed. Jason was grinning too. Dave and Marcia continued in their bewilderment. Although they had nothing but questions, they would later understand they had been given all the answers they needed.

<hr />

"Argentina?" Bartlett sat behind the big glass and wrought iron desk in what had been Belknap's office. Bartlett didn't feel particularly comfortable behind the desk, and he considered it a good thing that some of the more ostentatious assets would need to be sold off to help the company weather the storm of bad publicity and sluggish revenues.

Dave Whitman sat in one of the semi-circle of chairs in front of the great desk. He had just filled in Bartlett on the visit from the man called Josh.

"You know," said Bartlett. "The feds have a lot of good people trying to locate Belknap and his friends. So far they've turned up nothing. It gives one pause, doesn't it?"

"Yes it does," reflected Whitman. "Josh knew so much about my family. He even knew Brandi's name when she opened the door for him. He knew things about Belknap and the organization that would be nearly impossible for an outsider to find out. But he also seemed to have this sort of calmness or confidence or something—that made us want to trust him. Does that make any sense?"

Bartlett paused, swiveling his chair around to look out the panoramic window. "You know, I think it's a God thing. What do you think?"

Whitman gazed out the window as well. "I just can't come up with any other explanation. He didn't issue commands or make big predictions. He encouraged us. And he cooked us a darn good breakfast. He promised that Jason would be well someday, and that Belknap and the rest of them will see the consequences of their actions and maybe even change—if not in this world then certainly in the next."

Epilogue

I f you head east from Vancouver, Washington out into the Cascade foothills, and if you know where Camp Bonneville was once located, you can drive up the old road that was once accessible only to authorized military personnel. You'll drive up a little valley through a few miles of Douglas fir. Here and there you'll see evidence of decades of use by the U.S. Army—an occasional concrete foundation—an occasional rusted water tank.

Finally you'll come to the former conference and Retreat Center for the Wellness 120 organization. It's quite a bit different than it was a few years ago. Many of the ostentatious features are gone—such as the muscular statues of biblical characters and the helicopter landing pad. The grounds are not quite so immaculately maintained. But activity around the facility is no less evident. Wellness 120, as it liquidated assets, sold the site to a ministry that rehabilitates wayward inner-city youth. The auditorium, kitchen and dining hall still hum with life. Kids and counselors walk and run back and forth from their dormitories and cabins. On the peripheries of the facility, they are engaged in all sorts of activities: baseball, archery and wilderness survival skills. In one way, it's not unlike the summer camps that Tyler Belknap used to put on. In other ways, it's diametrically the opposite.

Across the parking lot, where a few cracks appear in the pavement, a cyclone fence still stands. Parts of it have been overgrown with the invasive Haines Ivy—not native to the Pacific Northwest. One such vine obscures an old gate. A rusted cardkey box pokes out of the vegetation. If you were athletic and adventurous, you could climb the gate. No security cameras would be there to attest to your presence.

On the other side, you would find yourself on an overgrown path. Hints of old pavement peek through the ground cover. You decide to make your way up what used to be a broad trail—large enough to accommodate a truck. The going gets tough as you pick your way through another invasive species, the Himalayan Blackberry. Ubiquitous in parts of the Pacific Northwest, it was brought here by settlers who wanted larger, sweeter blackberries then those yielded by the native plants. You can't help but notice that the berries on these particular plants are nearly twice as large as any you've seen, yet they're oddly misshapen. You are tempted to try one but something tells you to leave it alone. You begin to notice other plants along what's left of the trail. None of them look right. The ferns have strange, unfernlike appendages. The moss seems to have attached itself to everything, in a way that isn't normal for any moss you've known.

You notice that you're following a deep, narrow canyon to your left—choked with heavy vegetation—giant berry vines and those strange ferns. The cliff to your right becomes steeper and taller. You can hear a stream flowing below, but you can't see it—too much vegetation. You come to a second gate, nearly obscured by ivy, berry vines and another brown, fungusy-looking plant you can't identify. You've had to resort to using the large utility knife that you carried with you in the woods, to cut through the vegetation. You see that the lock has rusted off the gate, and with a good deal of pulling and cutting of vines, you open the gate enough to squeeze through.

Somewhere up ahead an animal is making an abrasive screeching. You think it might be a bird, but you can't be sure. This place is starting to give you the creeps. Even so, you move on through the denser and ever-darkening forest.

Finally, the canyon and the stream that formed it end in a sheer rock bulwark draped by a waterfall. The trail is at an end. By now the vegetation is so thick that it seems like twilight, even though it's two in the afternoon on a warm, sunny day. As your eyes adjust to the gloom, you discern what appears to be an opening in the rock wall on your right, framed by ponderous and weathered wooden beams. Just inside is a massive steel door, covered in peeling camo green paint. The door is shrouded with an alien-looking ivy, unlike any you've seen earlier in your trek. On closer examination, you discover the door is slightly ajar. Curious, you manage to insert a thick, fallen branch in the opening to use as a lever. The door is rusted so badly that it barely budges. The branch breaks and you find another, thicker branch. You continue pulling and breaking branches until, millimeter by millimeter, you have opened the door enough to squeeze in.

In the dark, musty interior, your flashlight reveals an empty chamber and a long corridor stretching away into blackness. Here, near the entrance, some type of grey mushroom-type organism has coated the wall. Peculiar white insects with abnormally large antennae scurry away from your feet, which, you reassure yourself, is much better than scurrying *toward* them.

You move down the corridor, shining your flashlight into each room you come to. Benign relics of some kind of office environment are scattered on the floor: a pencil, paper clips, a few old post-it notes, Cat5 cable plugs evenly spaced around the walls. Furnishings and equipment have long ago been taken away.

You keep walking. Finally, the corridor ends like the box canyon outside, except instead of a waterfall there's a single door in the otherwise featureless back wall. You try the doorknob and it opens. Inside is a small room lined with empty shelves. Curious about what may have been stored here, you scan your flashlight briefly over the shelves. Just as you conclude there's nothing interesting to see, you spot a small protuberance about five inches back under one of the shelves. You examine it. It's some kind of a button. You press it, and nothing happens. You wonder if the switch isn't corroded, so you press it repeatedly. The eleventh time, you hear a click followed by the grinding and squeaking of long-unused gears. You gasp as the shelves and wall suddenly roll aside to reveal what seems to be a richly furnished parlor. It occurs to you that whoever cleaned out the rest of this huge underground complex knew nothing about this secret.

You step over the threshold and gaze at the plush furniture, the bookshelves filled with collector's volumes, the art, the sculptures. The expansive room reminds you of the library of some exclusive club for wealthy old men in London. You notice that the room has three doors. You try one, and it opens into a luxury apartment. The other two doors open into similar rooms, and you decide to explore the largest. In the kitchen, you find a pantry full of freeze-dried foods, fine wines, liquor tanks of water. You wander into the bedroom, where there is huge four-post, king-size bed. A walk-in closet reveals a few items of clothing, on hangers as well as scattered on the floor, as if whoever lived here had beat a hasty retreat. A pair of men's slacks and a couple of shirts suggest a tall, lean man once owned them. A businesslike pantsuit that apparently belonged to a petite woman hangs nearby. Judging from that and the few toiletries left in the restroom, this apartment (unlike the others) had been occupied, or prepared for, a couple. In the corner of the bedroom you are surprised to see a ponderous safe. Its thick door is open, so of course you can't resist peeking inside. There's nothing — but a glint catches your eye. You look closer. On the floor of the safe are glittering tracks of some yellow metal. Whatever was once deposited here has been withdrawn.

⟹➤●◄⟸

Under the leadership of Clifford Bartlett and his team, Wellness 120 was transformed into a no-nonsense provider of reliable, quality foods and supplements. Its name was changed to Welllness (with three Ls to make it a unique name). Gone was all the hype, exaggerated claims and religious double-talk, and any implication that God had promised a particular lifespan to humans if they did all the right stuff.

It was not easy to explain all this to Welllness customers. Many of them had admired and followed Belknap as if he were God's official spokesman. Dawson Criswell was one such person. It took him a while to get through his disillusionment. Once he had made the journey, he was able to help employees and customers make the journey as well.

Bartlett offered Whitman the position of Operations Director, but Whitman knew where to draw the line. He was creative with management skills, not a manager with creative skills. He was happy and fulfilled as Creative Director. And with his son's condition, he didn't need the additional stress.

Of course everyone continued to wonder and speculate as to the whereabouts of Belknap and his cronies. The question dominated the news media for a few weeks, and then, like other news stories, it faded from the short public attention span, displaced by the antics of celebrities, politicians and preachers.

Marcia and Dave continued to struggle with their experience. More and more, they fell back on the words of Josh, which seemed to echo the words of Jesus. God's justice and God's grace would have the last word.

———————

About 10 miles outside of Buenos Aires, up a long road with a manned security gate, there is a compound of low-lying industrial buildings and warehouses. One, obviously the "front office," is an imposing, three-story glass and concrete structure with a sweeping, curved window overlooking a grove of jacaranda trees.

Inside the window, a tall, handsome sixty-something man sits at a wrought iron and glass desk. His feet are propped up and he reclines in his custom designed chair with his fingers laced behind his smoothly shaven head. He sports a thin mustache and a small beard on his chin. The fresh latte sitting on his desk is organic with a half-shot of butter rum flavoring. The business cards on his desk tell us he is Tiburon Belmontes, CEO of Rebosando de Salud, which roughly translates into "glowing with health."

He contemplates: *Life is damned good here in Argentina. God has blessed our work in ways that never would have been possible back in the States. It was a good thing I converted my millions into actual gold so many years ago. Our little stash of capital has survived the recession and has been essential in getting us around the heavy business regulations down here. Money, favors and political leverage can open nearly any door. And ol' Richardson is as effective at eliciting cooperation down here as he was back in the States. All we needed to make things work here was a little image tweaking to accommodate the Hispanic culture and the Catholic religious milieu—but wherever people are religiously trained, they will respond the same. Just tell 'em God will be happier if they do some-thing—the more difficult the better. Then give 'em some-thing to do, and (here's the crazy part) charge them mon-ey for it! Then sit back and watch the profits and power pile up.*

Yeah—the move and sneaking out of the States was a big hassle—but things were getting downright uncom-fortable back there—too many consumer protection laws. Here in Argentina, GMO laws are pretty much non-existent, or at least circumventable. But what do those government geeks know anyway? They're all afflicted with spirits of perversity—every last one of 'em! Which is why the world's GMOs are dangerous. We're the only ones who really know what we're doing. We've been work-ing with GMOs for over two decades back in the States—using them to improve flavors, enhance feelings of energy—even addicting people to our products.

Yessir—down here in Argentina we can really get into cutting-edge organic psychoactive substances—creating products that will nail the senior market world-wide with the prospect of enhanced memory—Eternal Recall—Recuerdo Eterno *we call it down here—and feelings of euphoric well-being. Heck—if they're lucky a few of 'em may even live to be 120 like the Lord intend-ed. One thing's for sure—it's a helluva lot easier to find human guinea pigs down here—and much easier to get rid of 'em if the tests turn out poorly, like what hap-pened with that Jason kid.*

Anyway, ponders Belmontes, a broad, cheesy grin spreading across his face, *things are so much easier here in Argentina. Life in these perilous end times can be good—really good!*

Acknowledgements

For decades I wanted to write fiction, but never got around to it. My father wrote and illustrated science fiction comic book stories in the 1940s. He also wrote short stories, scripts (and much later a narrative based on the Old Testament). Fresh out of college I thought, *I should write some fiction*, but I didn't. I went into graphic design and illustration, gradually oozing into writing promotional copy and print ads. Still no fiction. Another decade or two went by. My ordination compelled me to write sermons that wouldn't put people to sleep. Congregants fell asleep anyway and I still hadn't written any fiction.

I went back to college and wrote a thesis. I don't remember all the specifics right off hand, but I don't think it was fiction. Then I found myself writing magazine articles. None of them were fiction. As I neared the age when most people retire, my mental list of things that I had always wanted to do multiplied. Writing fiction was still there, but other things were taking a front seat.

Then one day my friend (of about 48 years) Greg Albrecht, longtime coworker and President of Plain Truth Ministries had a suggestion. "Why don't you write a short novel?" The more we discussed the idea, the more excited I got. Here it was at last, my chance to write fiction. I would have to "get around to it" because it would have deadlines. Plain Truth Ministries would publish it, and it would convey some important lessons about God's love and grace, the dangers of abusive religion and survival after religious bubbles burst.

What I didn't realize at the time was the massive life changes I would go through before the novel was finished. My wife of 42 years, Kayte, was battling ovarian cancer. She was delighted that I was undertaking the project, and I remember discussing with her the initial concept. Not long afterward, her cancer was found to be inoperable. In the months of adjustment following Kayte's death, I sat for an hour or two each day on my front porch with my laptop, grinding out early drafts of parts of this book.

Several months passed, and the book slowly took shape. Meanwhile, I became reacquainted with a good friend, Kaye, whom my late wife and I had known well in earlier years. Our friendship rapidly blossomed into love. Greg Albrecht, here in the Portland, Oregon area for a conference, took Kaye aside and made her promise to keep me working. She took the promise seriously. Accordingly, I wrote much of the book during our engagement while sitting on Kaye's sofa or on her back porch, with our combined grandkids thundering through the house. My laptop even went with us on our honeymoon.

Beyond that, Kaye's edits and suggestions proved vital. She is an avid reader—about one book a week. She pointed out things in the book that I thought were perfectly clear but in fact weren't (she pointed out other things outside of the book, but that's another story and that's what spouses are supposed to do).

My thanks to Greg for giving me this opportunity and his guidance along the way, to my late wife Kayte for her enthusiasm and positive support despite her devastating illness, and to my new wife Kaye for her practical insights and persistent motivation.

Singular thanks also goes to Katie McCoach, our developmental editor, especially for her help in shaping the characters (and getting rid of one, whom you'll never know about—just as well). Thanks to Laura Urista for her edits, suggestions and overall coordination and timing of the project. Thanks to Brad Jersak for his input and encouragement. Thanks to Dennis Warkentin for his work in promotion. Thanks to Deborah Wade and Mary Ellen Taylor of the FDA for their valuable information and perspective (what happens in the book may not be exactly how it would happen in real life—but this is, after all, fiction). And finally, thanks to Marv Wegner whose design expertise rendered the book legible and attractive.

Finally and foremost, my thanks goes to the Lord for walking through this with me and the team.

Monte Wolverton
Battle Ground, Washington
April, 2014